HOMANI TRIED

THE HOMANI SERIES
BOOK ONE

SARREN SCRIBNER

Copyright © 2022 Sarren Scribner

All rights reserved.

ISBN-EBOOK- 978-1-7781395-3-6

ISBN-PAPERBACK- 978-1-7781395-2-9

No part of this book may be reproduced in any form or by any electronic or mechanical means, including information storage and retrieval systems, without written permission from the author, except for the use of brief quotations in a book review.

This is a work of fiction. Names, characters, businesses, places, events, locales, and incidents are the products of the author's imagination or are being used in a fictitious manner. Any resemblance to actual persons, living or dead, or actual events is purely coincidental.

Cover Model - Brittany (Instagram @brittanynicolefougere)

Cover Design and Formatting - Elisabeth Garner/Books by E M Garner

CONTENTS

AUTHOR'S NOTE

Content Warning:
- Open door sexual content - consensual
- Forced confinement/physical abuse/torture
- Kidnapping
- Assault
- Emotional abuse
- Social alcohol consumption
- Medicinal drug use
- Poisoning
- Stalking
- Death

A huge thank you to my family for supporting me through this crazy process we call writing.

My husband, who loves me through my crazy.

My son and daughter, who knew to ignore me as I muttered to myself around the house as I worked out the plot.

My daughter in law, who literally saved my ass a thousand times through the editing process.

To my new friends I have made during this journey, your support has been invaluable.

Finally, to my readers, without your support, I would have no one to share my stories with. I love you all.

"Sometimes you will never know the value of a moment, until it becomes a memory."
- **Dr. Seuss**

HOMANI TRIED

CHAPTER

ONE

Calli's hand trembles slightly as she pulls the sheet of paper off the bulletin board.

Healthy females wanted for work - ages 21-35.

Calli thinks that sounds sketchy as shit, but the pains in her stomach from lack of food remind her of her limited choices for survival.

When had she eaten last? Was it two days? Three?

It didn't matter. She knows she will check out this ad and pray it is legit. Keeping her head down, she peers around her. The town looks a little better than most she has gone through in what used to be Northern British Columbia, cleaner, and the people she has seen seem to move with purpose, not defeat or desperation. She glances down at the paper again.

"Smiths Farm. Fanfuckingtastic. I'll be a farm hand or have my organs harvested for the black market," Calli chuckles under her breath. *Fuck it.*

"Neither," came the deep voice behind her.

Gasping and grabbing her chest, Calli whirls on the voice

and smacks her nose straight into a brick wall. Ok, not exactly a brick wall, but it sure felt like it. *Holy shit, that hurt.* Looking up, she can only see his teal blue eyes through her watering ones.

"You ok? I am so sorry to startle you." The wall apologized.

Holding her nose, she nods profusely like an idiot. Calli stares as her vision clears. Standing before her is the most gorgeous male specimen she has seen in all her years. At least six foot seven to her five foot seven, jet black hair, full sensual lips, firm jaw, and those damn eyes rimmed with the longest lashes. Not to mention that *body* - broad muscled chest, thick thighs, and multiple abs making their presence known through his form-fitting t-shirt.

Now, if I could just get him to turn around to check out his ass for the complete package.. wait, what? What the hell is wrong with me? Look at this guy; I feel like I could climb him like a tree and hump the bark off him. Whoa, girl, this is so not you.

"Miss, you ok?" Mr. Brickwall asks with concern.

Shit, now he thinks I'm crazy.

"Yeah, sorry, I was checking out your abs... I mean, this ad and you startled me. I'm good, thanks."

"You looking for work?"

"Depends on the work?" Calli retorts.

Tall, dark and climbable gives a small laugh. "Nothing too crazy, mostly house help."

He stuck out his hand. "Matt Smith."

She placed her smaller hand in his. "Calli, just Calli."

"It's a pleasure to meet you, Just Calli," he grins.

"So, I'm heading back to the farm." Matt gestures to the ad in her hand and raises his eyebrow.

Calli's confused. "Is this for a job interview?"

Matt leans against the bulletin board, slowly giving Calli a perusal from head to toe.

Damn, those eyes had her clenching her thigh muscles, feeling the inside getting wet. *I have got to stop this. Get it together, girl.*

Suddenly Matt's nostrils flare just a little, and a slight grin on the side of his mouth appears, bringing a downright dangerous dimple. "Oh, I think you'll be a fine candidate for the job."

CHAPTER

TWO

Leaning her head on the window of the battered pickup truck, Calli's gaze takes in the terrain outside the window. What was once lush fields are now dust spread out for miles.

Calli was a small child when the Great Release happened, and the world subsequently went to hell. Twenty-five years later, people are still trying to survive off what's left of the planet. Now only small colonies exist on the fringes of these wastelands.

Lost in her thoughts, Calli jolts back to the present when the truck quickly turns onto a side road. "How much further?"

"About a quarter-mile down this road to the farm's gates."

Squinting her eyes, she asks, "Is that green on the horizon? Do you have trees here?"

"You'll see."

Excitement building, Calli leans forward, her nose almost touching the windshield.

"Ohmygod ohmygod ohmygod," she exclaims as mountains and tall trees appear, surrounded by lush fields and a large stream running alongside. Calli hasn't seen such an oasis in years.

Drawing up to the gates, Matt waves at the heavily armed man at the guard post, who nods as he opens the gates for them. Matt drives the truck through.

"Are there more guards posted? There must be. People would fight over this," Calli breathes.

"Guards, electrified fencing, plus we have patrols. We like our privacy, but we also know how to defend what we have." Matt shrugs.

As they pass the fields, a few barns appear. Matt explains they're placed intentionally to house whatever equipment and supplies each crop requires.

The accommodations finally come into view. Cute little cottages surround what looked to be a small town. Swinging her head left and right, trying to take in the random shops, she spots a small school and what looks to be a town hall-medical clinic.

Calli's shocked by what she sees. Clean, well-fed, healthy families going about their daily lives. Shopping, chatting, laughing - like the world didn't pretty much end a quarter of a century ago.

Pulling up in front of a white cottage with a wraparound porch, Matt shut the truck off. "We're here."

"Is this where you live?"

"Yeah. Come on, grab your bag."

"I thought you lived on a farm?"

"This," he gestures to the whole town, "is Smith's farm."

"You want me to work for you? Here?"

"Yes. I need domestic help. Cooking, cleaning, I'm too busy trying to run this place and keep it from prying eyes.

Also, I hate to cook." Matt shrugs. "I know most colonies like to barter, but all I can offer you here is fresh food and a roof over your head."

"That's a better offer than I usually get," she laughs. Shouldering her bag, Calli rushes to catch up to Matt on the porch. Pausing as she walks through the front door, she drops her bag in stunned silence.

Gleaming hardwood floors cover the open space living-dining-kitchen concept. White cupboards with natural wood countertops give it a warm, inviting feel.

Overstuffed chairs with a matching leather couch face a stone fireplace in the living room area. A sizeable wooden dining room table, big enough to seat twelve, is next to the kitchen.

To the right is a staircase leading to the upstairs. Leaning to the side to peek, Calli counts three doors from where she can see through the upstairs open railing.

She turns to Matt in astonishment. "It's an actual home."

Chuckling, he says, "I should hope so. I built it."

Turning away to hide her expression, Calli murmurs, "I don't remember living in one."

Lightly touching her shoulder, Matt turns her to face him. The teal blue in his eyes briefly glitters turquoise. "Welcome home."

Calli squints at the brief change. A *trick of the light or lack of food,* she thinks with a shrug.

With a gentle squeeze on her shoulder, he motions her towards the stairs. "C'mon, let's get you settled into your room."

Matt stops at the door near the end of the hallway, "This will be your room," pointing to the door next to it, "That's the bathroom, and the door at the end is my room. If you need anything, make a list, and I'll get it picked up when there's a supply run if we don't have it in town." He nods as he heads back downstairs.

With a shaky hand, Calli opens the door to her room. Tears spring to her eyes as she takes in the large platform bed decorated with a colourful duvet and pillows. A tall dresser is in the corner. A large window bathes the room in natural light.

Overwhelmed with long-forgotten luxuries, Calli runs her hand over the duvet, feeling its pillow-like softness. Memories of constantly being on the run, living on the outskirts of one desolate area to the next with only thoughts of survival as her constant companion threaten to overwhelm her. The contrast between her past to this present is jarring. Sinking into the bed, she lets out a long sigh, closing her eyes.

CHAPTER

THREE

The blaring alarm jolts Calli out of bed. Heart racing, she looked around, disoriented in her surroundings; the day's memories came rushing back, giving her her bearings.

The long shadows in the room speak of time passing. Calli finds herself clumsy because of the fogginess of sleep. She stumbles out the door and down the stairs.

Calli finds Matt surrounded by blue smoke, jabbing a broom handle at the smoke alarm. On the stove sits a still-smoking charred casserole, the culprit of the current situation.

"Sorry I woke you," Matt says sheepishly. "I thought maybe you might be hungry, but..." He gestures to the black mess on the stove and then rubs the back of his neck. "I said I wasn't much of a cook."

She bites her lower lip to contain her laughter from bubbling up. "No, no, you were right. You need some, uh, help in the kitchen." Calli responds as she picks up the offending meal and dumps it in the nearby trash.

Opening the cupboards and taking stock, Calli looks over at Matt. "Give me a few minutes to familiarize myself with what you've got in here, and I should be able to whip something up."

She grabs some lunch meats, thick slices of bread and various kinds of cheese. Calli sets about making sandwiches. Spying a bag of homemade chips in the pantry, she adds those to the plate. Matt makes himself busy pouring glasses of iced tea and gathering napkins. Working comfortably together as a team, dinner is ready in no time.

Sitting across from Matt, Calli studies him as he bites into his sandwich. His deep, satisfying groan has her thighs clenching once again. *He makes eating look sexy, for fuck's sake.*

"You're not hungry?" Matt comments on her untouched food.

Caught once again fantasizing about her new boss, Calli quickly grabs a handful of chips and shoves them in her mouth.

"Starhveen," she says around a mouthful, chewing quickly. Swallowing, she repeats clearly. "I mean starving."

Calli leans forward, resting her elbows on the table. "So how did you build a town without a word getting out? Where are all these people from?" Calli rapidly fires her questions, her curiosity on overdrive.

Pushing back his chair and holding up his hands, Matt counters.

"Slow down. I have a few questions of my own. First, what were you doing this far out in the dead zone alone? You haven't been in any of the colonies that formed, or you wouldn't have been so shocked by what we have here." His eyes narrow with suspicion.

The banging of the door being thrown wide interrupts

their stare-off. A hulking blonde adonis rushes in, coming up short when he sees Calli.

"Matt, come quick. It's Maverick!" The adonis says urgently as he nervously glances in Calli's direction.

Scraping his chair back and grabbing a rifle by the door, Matt follows the man out, turning at the last minute to Calli.

"Stay put. I'll be back," Matt says sternly as he jumps into the waiting truck.

Alarmed and concerned, Calli makes her way onto the porch, peering down the street where the truck had disappeared.

Never one to be told what to do, she follows on foot to what looks like a gathering by the restaurant near the end of the street.

Out of breath from running, Calli gasps to the onlooker as she tries to catch her breath. "What's going on?"

Turning to Calli, the woman scrunches her nose. "New to town, are you?" Her stunning blue eyes narrow in suspicion, her question clearly rhetorical.

"Yes, I just arrived today," Calli says as she tries to peer around the woman who seems to be consciously blocking her view. Calli holds out her hand. "I'm Calli, Matt Smith's new housekeeper."

A wide smile appears on the woman's face, giving her features a stunning beauty. Her almond-shaped blue eyes light a little with excitement as she takes Calli's hand.

"Lilly. About damn time Matt brought in someone," Lilly says with a chuckle, running her hand through her long, silky, dark hair.

Still blocking Calli's view, Lilly glances over her shoulder and continues, "If you need anything, let me know, and I'll see what I can do. I own the supply store." Lilly nods at the building on the opposite side of the street.

A sudden roar sent vibrations through the surrounding air. BANG!

"What the fuck? Did they just shoot someone?" Calli exclaims as she tries to get around Lilly.

Grabbing Calli's arm with a steel grip to stop her, "Don't. Maverick will be fine. It was a tranquilizer gun. You're new here. This is town business." Lilly says as she stares Calli dead in the eyes. Then, with a nod, Lilly walks away, heading toward her store.

Calli notices the crowd has somewhat dispersed, leaving only herself and a few stragglers murmuring. Looking over to the restaurant, Matt and the blonde Thor look alike are carrying a dark-haired man between them, gently placing him in the back of the truck.

Matt stiffens and stares at Calli, his eyes narrow at the sight of her. Stalking toward Calli, she can see his bulging muscles straining against his t-shirt, taught with anger.

"I told you to stay put," he growls.

Rising up on tiptoes to gain some height, she plants her hands firmly on her generous hips. "If you would have asked, maybe I would have, but I don't like being told what to do by anyone," Calli grinds out, her temper flaring.

The world is suddenly upside down to Calli as Matt effort-lessly flings her over his shoulder. *What the actual fuck!*

"I'll be by to check on Maverick later, Jax," He calls over his other shoulder to the blonde guy.

Struggling to get down, Calli hears the bystanders chuck-ling at her predicament. A hand lands on her ample ass with a loud smack.

Calli lets out a screech, "Ho-How dare you!"

"How dare I?" Matt retorts, giving her ass two more stinging swats as he continues to carry her toward his house. "I told you to stay put for your own safety!"

Changing tactics, Calli calmly pleads. "Put me down, Matt. You're embarrassing me. Let's talk about this like two adults."

Not stopping until he reaches the porch, he gently puts Calli down. She immediately whirls on him, catching him off guard and kicking him in the balls. Matt groans and gasps for air, dropping to the ground and cupping his nether regions.

"Don't you ever lay a fucking hand on me again!" Calli yells as she stomps into the house and up to her room, leaving Matt on the front lawn.

The embarrassment of being manhandled and spanked in front of the town fuels her anger, and Calli slams the door to her room. *How fucking dare he!*

Flopping down on the bed, Calli weighs her options. She could pack up her things and leave. But, no, that would be a rash reaction. She's survived this long on her own, making well-thought-out decisions. Exhausted from running from one place to the next, she can't bring herself to leave just yet.

A soft knock on her door reminds her of her other issue - Matt.

"Calli, can I come in?" Matt says softly.

Sitting up, Calli sighs, "Fine."

Opening the door a crack, Matt hesitates. "You won't throw anything at me, will you?"

Calli rolls her eyes and waves him in.

Matt cautiously approaches the bed and sits next to her. Raising her gaze to him, she schools her facial features into a neutral expression. He sits on the bed beside her, rubbing his hands on his muscled thighs.

"I'm sorry I spanked you. You gave me everything that I deserved. I was trying to protect you, but you proved you can take care of yourself." He chuckles, covering his crotch for protection.

Feeling mollified by his apology, Calli turns to Matt on the bed. "I don't know what the big deal is. I just wanted to see if I could help."

"I appreciate that, Calli, but there are just some things about this town that I need to handle, and it was for your own safety-"

Calli interrupts, "Talk to me, Matt. If this is going to work, trust goes both ways."

Matt let out a long-suffering sigh. "I know, I know. Just give it time, okay? It's your first day here, and we don't bring in a lot of strangers. We just need to get to know you; as you said, this place is different. The townsfolk here are suspicious of new people. "

When he shifts towards her, their faces are mere inches apart. "We need to protect the farm as best we can." Matt ends in a whisper.

Calli stares into Matt's eyes, quietly regarding him for a minute, trying to get her sudden arousal under control. The desire in his eyes matches hers.

"I get it, and I know this place is so much different from the outside world. It's survival of the fittest out there. I've survived this long; I can take care of myself."

Matt cocks his head to the side, and a curious expression crosses his face. "How have you not seen any other towns like this? There are colonies all along the coast. So why are you going to the outskirts? Is there something I should know, Calli? Are you in trouble?"

Calli looks down, shifting slightly away from him. "No, no,

Matt. I'm not in trouble. It's just the way it's always been for me. It's always been safer to be on the outside. I didn't realize - I never thought I could settle down or have a home. It wasn't how I was raised." she says with a slight shrug.

After sitting silently for a while, Calli sheepishly looks at Matt. "I'm glad I found this place."

"I'm glad you're here, too," he grins.

The proximity of them being so close, feeling the heat from Matt's body mere inches away from her, stirs a desire in Calli. A flash of heat courses through her, her skin tingling with sensation; Calli squeezes her thighs together, trying to soothe the sudden throbbing between her legs.

Matt stiffens beside her, his nostrils flaring slightly. Glancing down, Calli notices his shoulders are not the only thing that's stiff right now.

Oh, wow! By the size of the bulge in Matt's jeans, he would definitely not disappoint.

So what is it about this guy? She muses. *One minute I want to strangle him; the next minute, I want to fuck him.*

Matt lets out a low groan as he slowly stands up. "I'll let you get some sleep," he says as he tries to adjust the bulge in his pants without her noticing.

Pausing at the door, Matt glances at her over his shoulder with desire burning in his eyes. "Sleep well, Calli. My room is down the hall if you need me for anything."

Flustered at the double meaning, Calli nods, fearing if she opens her mouth, she'll ask him to stay the night.

CHAPTER
FOUR

Morning arrives with the early glow of sunrise filtering through the windows. The long warm rays on her face cause Calli to stretch out of her slumber.

Calli lies in bed thinking about the events of the day before. First, she was furious with him for slapping her ass the way he did. Then, the sting of his hand plays in her mind. That nice burn sends tingles down her whole body.

Calli slowly rubs her hand over the skin where Matt had spanked her. Still feeling the imaginary sting, her nipples harden. Running her fingers up her side, she reaches for her full breast. Pinching and tweaking the nipple elicits a moan from her. Her other hand slowly moves between her legs, her finger rubbing small circles over her clit and then dipping inside her channel.

Picturing Matt in her head, she inhales deeply through her nose, catching his woodsy scent, which is still faint in the room. His eyes, those full lips. She increases the pace with her fingers arching her back as a fine, sheer film of sweat covers her body. Her release building, Calli's imagination runs wild with visions of him reaching down to pluck her nipple into his mouth.

She can almost feel his hands on her skin, his warm mouth sucking on her flesh. Shaking and tight with tension, she lets out a long moan as her body explodes with her release.

Calli leans back on the covers, content in the afterglow of a long overdue orgasm. She wonders if she should pursue the attraction she has for Matt. If his heated glances are anything to go by, he wants her, and she wants him, but she is living under his roof. Not to mention the fact that he is her boss. Can they work past that and have a working relationship with benefits? She definitely wants the benefits. So, casual sex it is.

With a slight smile and shake of her head, Calli gets up from the bed and wanders into the shower. Decision made. It's time to start this new day.

Calli walks into the kitchen and sees Matt standing beside the island with a cup of coffee. "How'd you sleep?"

"Oh! Good, good." Calli blushes, her morning 'self-care' still fresh in her mind. *He couldn't have heard me, right?*

As if reading her thoughts, Matt gestures toward the coffee with a knowing grin. "I hope you like it intense; it's the only way I know how to make it."

Mouth agape, Calli stumbles over and grabs herself a coffee. Bringing the cup to her mouth with both hands to hide her expression, she swallows the nectar of the gods. "Mmmm, that's perfect." She chuckles. "So, what's on the agenda for today?"

Matt places his empty mug in the sink. "Well, I have to check on a few things with Jax. If you want to look around and take stock of what you need, you can head over to Lilly's store to get supplies. If she doesn't have it, she can order it. Tell her to put it on my tab."

"Okay. About Jax - are you going to be checking on... What was his name? Maverick?"

His teasing expression fades. Matt glares at Calli. "Don't worry about it. I need to take care of some things." He turns to walk out the door.

Calli quickly grabs his arm and he looks down at her hand. "I'm not being nosey. I was concerned."

Plucking her hand from his arm, Matt lets out a frustrated grunt. "Just let it go, Calli, please?"

Calli shakes her head and reminds him. "Trust works both ways, Matt."

When he didn't respond, Calli throws her hands up in exasperation. "I'll get back to work, boss!" She sarcastically salutes him.

FIVE

Matt jams his key in the ignition of the beat-up half-ton, angry at Calli's persistence. Driving through the main street, he lets out a frustrated sigh. His thoughts wander to when he first saw her staring at the ad he had placed.

Her red hair gleamed in the sun, and her green eyes had held such sadness. Calli's ample curves would bring any man to his knees, willing to worship the eternal bounty her body provides. Yet, his immediate attraction to her is both problematic and welcome.

One whiff of her scent, and he knows she is his mate. His immediate reaction is all the evidence he needs. His inner wolf pushing at him to claim her.

The problem, he muses, *is whether the townsfolk will accept her, or better yet, will she accept him?*

Adjusting the tightness in his jeans, Matt recalls this morning's events. Calli thought she was quiet, but he could hear clearly what she had been doing with his sensitive hearing. Every moan, gasp, her slight intake of breath while she was pleasuring herself, was as loud to him as if he was in the room. It took all of his willpower not to run up the stairs and ask to join in.

Shifting his focus to the day ahead, Matt steers his truck toward the last barn at the end of the property. Pulling up front, he parks by the big barn doors, noticing Jax already waiting for him outside.

"How's he doing?" Matt asks, nodding towards the barn.

Leaning against the red wooden exterior with his hands in his jeans pockets, Jax slowly shakes his head. "Maverick seems to get worse and worse. He's losing the battle with his animal. I'm worried."

Matt rakes his fingers through his hair in frustration. "Fuck!" he says. "We don't need this right now, especially with someone new in town. If his animal gets loose, if he loses control, people could get hurt."

Jax glances back at the barn. "I know you don't want to put him down, Matt, but some people just didn't come back right from those facilities. We all went through hell, but Mav," he pauses, "the scientist seemed to have it out for Maverick."

Matt leans against the barn, his mind wandering back to his time spent in the government facilities that had housed the horrors of the experiments. In the high-security blackout sites, the government used animal DNA, genetic splicing, and biomedical engineering to make the perfect soldier, morals be damned.

No one knows for how long, but in secret labs all over the globe, they created the Homogenous-Animalia, or as they labeled them, the Homani. Faster, stronger, more intelligent - deadly, even to each other.

"I can fucking hear you, you cocksuckers!" Maverick

bellows from inside the barn, jarring Matt back to the present.

Matt and Jax share a look, then Matt moves first, approaching the barn doors. "Let's get this over with." Jax reluctantly follows behind him.

The barn's interior is dimly lit. Maverick's tied with heavy chains to the back wall, anger rolling off him in waves. He struggles against his restraints when Matt and Jax come into view. "You don't have the fucking balls to put me down!" he spits toward them.

Matt looks at his longtime friend, heartbroken. He studies Maverick's face, searching for a glimpse of the young boy who always had a mischievous grin and a quick laugh. This was before the scientists took him away to be segregated from the rest of the Homani for their particular experiment.

He knew that what came back from the locked room wasn't the Maverick he knew, but a half-feral monster. So Matt had to do everything he could to help, rehabilitate, and hopefully save him.

"Maverick, listen to me," Matt says sternly. "The only way I can let you out of those chains is if you take the light sedative that Lilly's been making for you. You've come so far, but you know you're not in control without the meds."

Looking up, Maverick mocks Matt, "Oh poor Mav, better keep him on his meds like a good little boy so we can control him. Don't you think they have controlled me enough? Haven't I been through enough hell? Maybe the beast needs to be free. Did you ever think of that, Matt? Did you ever think that maybe we are more animals than humans?"

Jax raises both hands. "This isn't just for your safety but for the town's safety. You couldn't live with yourself if you hurt Lilly or one of the younglings."

Jax had hit the mark by mentioning the younglings. For all of Maverick's rage, he is still a protector of the children of this town.

Slumping in defeat, Maverick glances up at Matt. "I'll take the meds," he hisses.

Jax walks over to the side table where a syringe lays and gently injects Maverick in the thigh. Maverick's body immediately relaxes.

Working together, Jax and Matt remove the shackles from Maverick and let him out of the barn. "Lilly will have your injection for next week, Mav. So stick with the appointments, okay?"

Drawing a deep breath through his nostrils, Maverick tilts his head curiously to the side. His eyes widen briefly, flashing turquoise and then narrow.

"Sure, Matt. I won't miss my appointment," Mav says slowly as he climbs into Jax's truck.

CHAPTER
SIX

Calli slams another cupboard door, scrunching her face. She mimics Matt. "It's none of your business, Calli. You ask too many questions, Calli."

Yeah, well, maybe I don't have all the social skills, and perhaps I have some things I need to work on, but it's who I am. You try living out there on the run all your life, never really able to settle down, always looking over your shoulder.

Calli slumps down on the kitchen floor, drawing imaginary circles on the hardwood with her finger.

Okay, she sighs. *Mama taught me a lot of things. How to survive, how to fight, and how to lie low. But she never taught me how to talk to people or interact.*

It was always just her and Calli, abandoned building after abandoned building, always avoiding the colonies. Interaction with people was only out of necessity. Those interactions were few and far between, only occurring if they needed supplies. As she got older, if she had a sexual itch she wanted scratched, she'd venture to the outskirts, keeping her trysts brief and impersonal.

After her mama died, Calli kept up the old habits ingrained in her as a child, always yearning for a home.

Shaking off her pity party, Calli returns to work, takes stock in the kitchen and notes what she needs to pick up. Then, grabbing her jacket, she heads out the door walking towards Lilly's shop near the end of the street.

The outside of the store reminds Calli of a description she read in an old western novel she had found in one of the abandoned buildings she and her mom had lived in. Long flat roof, with two large picture windows displaying the ware that was for sale. The sign above the large double doors simply stated 'Lilly's'.

A bell chimes as she walks through the doors. Calli pauses and glances around, taking in the stock on the shelves. It has the basic staples: flour, sugar, salt, and dried meats. To the left are bins of various fruits and vegetables in season. In the center of the store overlooking all the aisles, there is a large square counter where Lilly stands talking to a few customers purchasing their supplies.

Lilly glances up at the sound of the bell. She was ringing out the last customer.

"What did that jackass do now?" she asks, seeming to read Calli's troubled expression.

Calli shrugs her shoulders. "I don't know. We both just seem to run hot and cold. He thinks I ask him too many questions, and he doesn't answer fuck all. Maybe it's just me; I'm not good with people."

Lilly leans on the countertop. "Matt has a lot on his plate and a good heart, but sometimes that boy's got a stick up his ass. He just needs a good woman to pull it out and smack him over the head with it, if you ask me." she laughs.

Calli chuckles with a gleam in her eye. "Maybe you're right."

Lilly straightens. "So, what can I do for you?"

Calli rattles off her mental list of things the house needs. Lilly turns and lifts the half door of the counter as she makes her way down the aisles, picking up Calli's order. Calli leans her back against the counter and waits.

The bell above the door grabs Calli's attention, and a dark-haired man walks into the store. She recognizes him as the man from yesterday - the one they'd dragged out sedated. Maverick, she thinks he's called.

Noticing Calli, Maverick pauses; his body stiffens. His eyes search out Lilly.

"Hey, Mav," Lilly calls out. "You're looking no worse for wear."

Maverick's eyes briefly fall back on Calli. A look of mistrust etches his features. His muscles bunch as he seems to grow larger.

Lilly rushes to him and lays a calming hand on his arm. "Hey, the boys fix you up, okay?" she inquires.

Shaking off his tension, he turns his attention to Lilly. "Yeah, I'm good."

He stares once more at Calli. With a nod, he turns around and walks out the door.

Calli lets out a breath she didn't realize she was holding as the tense moment dissipates.

"What was that about?" she asks Lilly.

Lost in thought, Lilly murmurs, "I don't know."

She stares at Mavericks retreating back. Shaking off the awkward scene, Lilly turns to Calli. "Do me a favour, okay? Maverick's going through some things right now. He's a good man, but he has trust issues with new people, so for the time being, avoid him."

Calli opens her mouth, but Lilly holds up her hand. "No questions on this, Calli. Just trust me, okay?"

She nods and gathers the bags that Lilly had brought to the counter.

"Matt said to put this on his bill," Calli says as Lilly walks her to the door, rubbing her back comfortingly.

"Will do," Lilly replies. "You concentrate on that stick we discussed," she says with a laugh, trying to bring light to the whole situation.

"If you need anything else or just wanna talk, you know where I'm at," Lilly smiles.

Calli looks at Lilly for a long time. When she speaks, there is a wealth of emotion behind her words. "I'd like that, a friend."

Back at the house, Calli puts away the groceries, chops up some vegetables and puts a pot roast in the oven. Then, setting the timer, she climbs the stairs and heads to the bathroom to run the water for the tub. A long soak sounds heavenly as she strips off her clothes.

The steam in the air from the water already has Calli's muscles relaxing. She cautiously steps into the hot water, letting it soothe her. Then, with her long, auburn locks piled on top of her head, she leans back, closing her eyes.

SEVEN

Matt is weary when he walks to the front door. Cooter and Johnson, the two elderly gentlemen who look after the hydro dam that kept the power running in the town, had noticed an oil slick on the water and had to shut down a turbine for maintenance.

Having gone to Brook's hardware store to source a part, he was told she might have to send somebody to one of the other communities and barter for it. Hopefully, someone will be able to supply it.

After checking on the fields and checking in with the farm hands, he's exhausted. There always seems to be something to do, or that needs to be fixed. Someone always has a question, but he doesn't have all the answers.

Matt loves this community they built and is proud of it and its people. But, sometimes, he just wants to shut the door and enjoy the quiet.

The timer in the kitchen dings. Matt notices it is too quiet in the house. *Was Calli here?* Drawing a deep breath, he could faintly smell her vanilla and lavender scent. Following his senses, they led him upstairs.

The door to the bathroom stands slightly ajar. Stepping in, Matt notices her lounging in the tub, her fiery red hair piled on top of her head in a messy bun, tendrils curling down along her cheeks and shoulders, floating lightly on the water.

Her soft, creamy skin peeked out from the bubbles covering the top of the water, stopping just below her breasts. Matt instantly hardens at the sight of her pink nipples peaking just above the water, almost teasing him with their supple points.

Calli's eyes are closed, adorable little snores escaping. She was asleep.

Feeling uncomfortable catching her in such an intimate moment, Matt quickly tries to backtrack his way out the door. But, unfortunately, he inadvertently knocks the brush off the counter in his hasty retreat.

Startled out of her slumber, Calli sits up with a gasp, immediately covering her breasts from his gaze.

"What are you doing in here?" she exclaims, embarrassed.

Matt holds his hands up as he walks back to the door.

"I'm so sorry I didn't know you were in here. I went looking for you and found you asleep. I, I didn't mean to invade your privacy. Your buzzer went off."

"My, what did what, now?" Calli furrows her brow in confusion.

"Timer for dinner? It went off, so I came looking for you." Matt says sheepishly.

Relaxing a little, Calli looks Matt up and down. "Well, you definitely found me," she smirks.

The heat in the bathroom rose, and it wasn't from the tub. Matt stares at her.

"Do you need a hand?" He asks, taking a more relaxed stance, leaning against the door frame.

Shifting slightly in the tub, Calli motions to the cloth with her head. "You could do my back." She replies as she winks at him.

Like a flash, Matt is at the side of the tub kneeling, cloth in hand, as he dips it in the water letting the back of his hand trail on her leg and outer thigh before bringing up the fabric and placing it on her back.

He washes her from shoulder to shoulder down her side using slow, circular, sensual motions. Next, he trails her upper spine, repeating the process on the other side.

Calli's breathing increases and Matt can hear her heartbeat pounding in her chest.

Rinsing off her back, "Can I do the rest of your body?" his voice is low and husky with desire.

Calli turns towards him; her cheeks flush with arousal as she nods. Matt sits back on his heels and slowly removes his shirt.

"I don't want to get this wet." He places it on the chair as he stares at her with desire.

Biting her lower lip, Calli's gaze zeros in on his washboard abs, trailing down to the V that hints at the top of his waistband.

Matt places both hands on each side of the tub, leaning forward. He growls in her ear, "I'm going to touch you, I'm going to savor you, then I'm going to devour you."

Calli gasps out, "I want you. I want all of you."

Matt's mouth hovers above her lips. "I want you, too," he whispers just before covering his mouth with hers.

Calli's body is on fire from Matt's kiss, his lips demanding her soul. Their tongues meet, stroking one another as passion ignites between them. Matt's hand grasps the back of her neck while the other explores her breast.

Never breaking the kiss, his powerful hands knead her ample bosom, tweaking and pinching her nipples between his fingers. The pleasure-pain drives Calli to new heights. His hand slowly works its way over her soft stomach, stopping briefly to squeeze and massage.

Pulling back from the kiss, Matt stares into Calli's eyes. "Fuck, you're gorgeous. A man could get lost in your curves. You have the body of a goddess, soft and welcoming. You were built for sex."

"Then fuck me." Calli gasps.

Lifting her out of the tub, Matt carries her into the bedroom and lays her on the bed. "Oh, I plan to, Calli. You're mine."

He slowly runs the tips of his fingers up the inside of her leg from ankle to thigh, stopping just mere inches from her aching mound. "You've been a good girl, haven't you? Good girls get rewarded," he says with a smirk.

"Yes!" Calli begs.

Opening the drawer by the bed, Matt grabs two belts and looks at her for permission. She nods eagerly. He takes her ankles and spreads her legs, looping the leather over one, then the other, securing them to the posts at the edge of the bed. Leaving her open and available for his pleasure. Kissing each quivering thigh, he looks at Calli and whispers, "Hold still."

Lowering his mouth, he licks her outer folds with the flat of his tongue. Calli's upper body arches off the bed, her hands looking for purchase in the sheets to cling to. "I said, hold still," he growls, using his forearm to brace her.

Sliding his thumb into her channel, he spreads her inner lips and continues his assault on her pussy. Then, feeling her tension build as her body shakes, desperate for release, he raises his head. "Don't, Calli. I didn't give you permission to come yet."

"Please," Calli begs, fat tears of frustration dripping on the sheets below her, "I need -"

Lowering his head once more, Matt soothes, "I know, baby, you will."

Delving back between her legs, Matt pulls her swollen clit into his mouth and sucks hard, causing a squeal from Calli.

Matt raises his hand and covers her mouth, keeping her moans a hush until she has permission to scream her release.

Eyes meeting, Matt swirls his tongue around her clit then flattens it to the roof of his mouth, his thumb stroking the swollen spot inside her channel- pulling back, he removes his jeans, climbing on the bed, his long, thick cock positioned at her entrance.

Surging forward into her wet pussy, he commands, "Now, Calli," as he sets a punishing pace. "Fuck, you're so tight."

Overwhelmed with the feeling of fullness, her need burning like fire through her, her release barrels towards her. Calli explodes around his cock, screaming her release. Her orgasm, a vice-like grip on his cock, sets off his own release.

"Good girl," Matt says as he gently kisses her forehead.

EIGHT

Over the next few days, Calli takes pride in her new home. Bringing in fresh flowers from the back garden, she adds little feminine touches to the house.

Matt, noticing Calli's effort, asks over coffee, "How about you and I take a break from work today?"

"Really?" Calli beams.

"Yeah, I think the town can survive without us for one day." He chuckles as he gathers her in his arms. "How about we go to the lake? I can show you the beautiful beach we have here."

Calli looks down at the floor. "Um, I don't have a bathing suit," she says with regret.

Matt laughs. "That's perfect! Skinny dipping, it is!" He fist pumps the air and lets out a whoop like a teenager.

As they drive down a gravel road, Calli notices some children playing in the woods, darting in and out between the trees.

"Hey, Matt? Should those kids be out here?" she asks with concern.

Glancing in the direction Calli is pointing, Matt pulls the truck over and shuts off the engine. Calli follows him as he gets out of the truck.

A streak of motion catches Calli's eye just as three young children tackle Matt. Rolling on the ground, the children's peals of laughter echo in the woods as Matt tackles and tickles each child.

Calli's heart swells at the sight of Matt's roughhousing with the children. His laughter mixes with theirs. She hasn't seen this side of Matt, so carefree and playful. It suits him.

A low growl halts their play as Maverick rounds the corner of the truck.

"Oh shit, Matt, sorry. I didn't see you there," Maverick apologizes as the children surround him. They hang off him like a human jungle gym.

Matt chuckles as he walks over to Calli. "Mav teaches the kid's survival skills," he says. "As you can see, they love him." He gestures to Maverick, who is trying to pry the younglings off of him.

"What are you doing out here?" Maverick asks.

Matt glances at Calli. "We took the day off, so I'm going to show her the beach." Matt's eyes widen. "Uh, yeah. You might want to keep the younglings away from there for a bit."

"Why?" Maverick asks, then quickly says, "Oh. Oh! Yup, will do!" He winks at Matt as he gathers his group and heads in the opposite direction.

"Matt!" Calli blushes. "You basically just told him we were going to have sex!"

Matt answers her. "Am I wrong?" Giving Calli a smoldering look over his shoulder.

Calli rolls her eyes. "Well, no. But you didn't have to announce it."

Leading Calli to the beach on foot, Matt holds branches aside for her.

"Maverick seems interesting. I wouldn't have pegged him as the kid-friendly type," Calli hedged, looking at Matt.

Matt gives Calli a boyish grin. "Mav. He can appear gruff, but underneath? He's a big softie for kids," he says as he carefully guides her through the path to the lake.

"I've known him all my life. Saved each other's asses more times than I can count." Matt shakes his head. "Once he warms up to you, he's a solid friend."

The path opens up ahead of them. The sunlight shimmers off the water, inviting them to play in its waves. As he bounds towards the water, Matt tosses Calli on his shoulder.

"Matt! Don't you dare get me wet!" she screeches.

She got a light swat. "I thought that was the whole point," he says with a cheeky grin.

He slowly lets Calli down, stopping just shy of the water's edge. Their arms wrap around each other, and Matt leans in. His lips barely touch hers as his tongue teases her mouth open. Calli breathes out a sigh as their tongues meet. Her hands tighten on his broad shoulders as a rush of desire burns through her. His rough stubble grazes her cheek as he slowly kisses his way down her neck. Bunching his shirt in her hands, Calli tugs, needing to feel his skin against her. Pulling back, they strip off their clothes. Matt stares at Calli, his eyes darkening with desire as he approaches her.

Holding up a hand, Calli stops him. "I hope you're feeling creative," she says as she glances at the sand beneath them. "That," she points to the sand, chuckling, "and lady bits don't mix."

"The lady wants creative, does she?" Matt smirks as he lifts her up, placing her legs on his broad shoulders and burying his face between her thighs.

Briefly marvelling at his strength, Calli's head immediately empties of thought when his tongue delves deep inside her. Sucking and teasing, as his mouth and teeth bring a sudden orgasm crashing through her. Holding the back of Matt's head, Calli's body shivers from the unexpected release.

Setting her back on her feet, Matt gives her a tender kiss. "Was that creative enough for you?"

Calli glances up at Matt through her lashes. "Two can play that game," she says as she lowers to her knees on the soft sand.

Matt's cock bobs with the weight of his erection. A vein pulses along its length as pre-cum fills the slit at the end. Calli licks the head, savouring Matt's flavour as she slowly works him down her throat. Matt grunts out a satisfying sound as she wraps her small hand around his base, stroking upward as she takes him deeper. Mouth stretched wide, Calli breathes through her nose on her downward stroke, catching a breath when she can. She hollows out her cheeks as she sucks him down, swirling her tongue around his tip as she hums with her pleasure.

Matt's hands caress Calli's silken strands, his hips thrust forward as he watches Calli's breasts bounce with each stroke. His erratic pace and moan of pleasure are the only warning Calli has before a burst of warmth slides down her throat. Licking him clean, Calli gives the tip a gentle kiss before she rises to face him.

Matt gives Calli a satisfied smile. "Touché, Calli. Touché."

Gathering their clothes, Matt holds Calli in his arms as they watch the sunset on the lake.

CHAPTER

NINE

As time passes, Calli and Matt fall into a comfortable routine. Matt oversees the town, and Calli handles the domestic duties of running the house. At dinner, their conversation flows easily about their day, and they fill their nights with passion.

Sitting on the front porch with a cup of coffee, Calli mulls over her situation with Matt. Having never been in one spot for too long, this would be her first long-time fling. She enjoys the time she's spending with him. How Matt makes her coffee in the morning, or runs a tub for her at night, adding her favourite oils. She loves how he checks on her through the day to see if she needs anything, or to just hear her voice. A small smile grazes her lips at the memories. He makes her feel cared for, pampered. Sitting forward Calli's mouth opens in a silent O. Oh shit. It's a relationship. The word relationship gives her pause when it pops into her head. As shocking as it is, it makes some sort of sense as her feelings for Matt have gone beyond lust.

Looking inward, Calli realizes her feelings for Matt are

more than lust. It's love. Panicking at the thought, Calli abruptly stands up, spilling her coffee with the sudden movement. Then, rushing into the kitchen to deposit her cup in the sink, she quickly washes her coffee-soaked hands and heads out the door to see the only person she can talk about this to - Lilly.

Bursting through the shop doors, Calli catches her breath. Her anxiety and impromptu cardio suffocating her. Looking around wildly, she spots Lilly stocking shelves.

"Lilly," she gasps out.

Rushing to Calli's side, Lilly's face is drawn with concern. "What's wrong? What happened?" she fires at Calli as she ushers her to a nearby chair.

Lilly gently takes her hands, squatting down in front of Calli, "Breathe, girl. Deep breaths."

Staring into Lilly's bright blue eyes, Calli bursts into tears. "I - I think I love him!" she exclaims.

Then, falling back on her ass, Lilly bursts into a fit of laughter. "Oh dear god, is that what got you in a tizzy?" Lilly says as she wipes the tears from her own eyes. "Girl, this whole town can see that! Are you just figuring this out now?" she peels off into another fit of giggles.

Shocked, Calli straightens in her chair. "But I've never been in love before!" she says as she covers her face with her hands. "Am I that obvious? What if he doesn't feel the same way?" Calli's face pales with mortification as she swats a still-laughing Lilly on the floor. "You need to help me. What should I do?"

Gaining control of her mirth, Lilly once again takes Calli's hands. "Calli, look at me. Although I've known Matt most of my life, I have never seen him truly happy until you arrived here. That man worships the ground you walk on. Tell him how you feel. Sometimes we need to use our words." Lilly says as she waggles her eyebrows suggestively. "Lord knows, half the town can hear you two communicating in the bedroom, loudly."

Embarrassment riding her hard. Calli covers her now red face. "Oh, fuck me," she says.

"Yeah, we've heard that one," Lilly quips, "quite a bit." Then she busts out in a fit of giggles.

"Wait, how can anyone hear us unless they're outside our house?" Calli narrows her eyes at Lilly. "I'm not *that* loud."

All humor left Lilly's face. "I think it's time you and Matt have a serious talk, Calli," she says as she gets up off the floor and dusts off her jeans.

Calli swears she hears Lilly mutter something about kicking Matt's ass.

"Hear what he has to say, and Calli? Never doubt that man's love for you, okay? No matter what." Lilly says with unease as she gets back to work, dismissing Calli.

MATT CLIMBS the front porch steps, and the smell of fresh baked beans and homemade brown bread with molasses hangs in the air. His stomach grumbles at the delicious aroma.

Over at the couch, he notices Calli is sound asleep. Quietly sitting beside her, he gently gathers her in his arms. She briefly stirs, then snuggles into his chest.

Breathing in her scent of lavender and vanilla, Matt closes his eyes and thanks whatever God is out there for bringing her into his life. As if sensing his presence, Calli slowly awakens and smiles at Matt. "Oh, you're early," she says groggily.

"Yeah, I wanted to get home so I could hold you," he replies, kissing the top of her head.

Elation fills Calli, then thoughts of her talk with Lilly remind her of a conversation that needs to be had. Pulling back slightly from Matt, Calli drops her eyes. "Matt, we need to talk."

Shifting nervously on the couch, Calli continues, "I- I don't know where this is heading with us, Matt. I spoke with Lilly today, and she seemed quite upset that you're holding something back from me."

Matt stiffens, and his eyes glitter. "What exactly did Lilly say to you, Calli?"

"Nothing really, just that we need to talk."

Letting out a heavy sigh, Matt looks down at his hands. "She's right. It's time I told you the truth."

Calli leans forward and grasps Matt's hand. "What truth?" she asks.

"It's time I told you what we are, who we really are," he shifts nervously.

"What are you talking about, Matt?" Calli asks in trepidation as prickles of fear go down her spine.

Still clasping her hand, he turns towards her. "I don't know what you remember from before the Great Release. You would've been a child. So many stories have been told and retold that the truth is muddled in the middle. What do you know about the Homani?" he asks.

Wide-eyed, Calli stares at him. "I - I know that there were horrible experiments done on children and people, that sick scientists changed their DNA and created a hybrid human. I know that they died when the bombs dropped, and life went to shit," she ends in a whisper.

Raising her chin with one finger to look her in the eyes, Matt says, "They survived, Calli. We, this community, are the Homani."

Jerking back from Matt, "No! That can't be true," Calli exclaims, fear gripping her. "My moth... they said you were all dead!" Calli jumps off the couch and puts her hands up in front of her. Rising slowly, Matt reaches out to her, but Calli flinches.

"Calli, you have nothing to fear. We won't hurt you. *I* could never hurt you," Matt pleads.

Still backing closer to the stairs, Calli cries, "Stay back! I gotta go. I can't stay here - I can't be here," she says frantically.

"Calli, for fuck's sake, I love you. Nothing will change that. Don't you love me too?" Matt asks in a pain-filled voice.

With deep sadness, Calli looks at Matt. "You can't love me, Matt. I'm not worthy of you or your love," she mumbles as she walks up the stairs to pack.

Calli heard the door slam, and a loud, mournful howl filled the sky, shaking the house. Then it all clicks into place.

The changing of the eye colour, the extraordinary strength, the secrecy. Her heart shatters. *How could I be so stupid? I've fallen in love with the one man that will despise me.*

With tears streaming down her face, Calli fills her backpack, not noticing the yellowed newspaper clipping that falls to the floor, and walks out the front door.

CHAPTER

TEN

Matt stomps into the bar. Glancing around, he notices Maverick in the corner, nursing a beer. Matt gives him a curt nod before turning towards the bar top, the wood creaking when he sits on a vacant stool. Raising two fingers, he gestures to the bartender, "Jameson, neat and keep them coming."

The young bartender raises his eyebrows at Matt's demeanor but knows better than to comment. "Coming right up, Matt," he says. He hurries away to get Matt's drink.

"What's got you in a tizzy?" Jax says as he sits beside Matt, clapping him on the back.

Matt turns and glares at him; his eyes are bright turquoise. "Don't fuck with me today, Jax.".

Raising both hands in surrender, concern etching his face, Jax quietly sips his drink, giving him the time he needs.

Two drinks later, Matt notices movement to his left as Lilly sits down on the empty barstool next to him. She motions to the bartender for a vodka and tonic and then turns to Matt. "So, you royally fucked it up, didn't you?"

Matt's muscles tense, and his eyes flare turquoise. "You just had to push it, didn't you, Lilly? She wasn't ready."

"Oh, don't give me that shit, Matt. She was more than ready, and it was way overdue for her to know the truth." Lilly counters.

"Yeah, well, she fucking left!" Matt growls at Lilly.

Jax leans forward. "What the fuck do you mean, she left?"

"She left. Are you both fucking deaf?" Matt raises his voice.

The patrons in the bar go quiet, not used to seeing Matt so close to beast mode. Glancing around, Matt lowers his voice. "I told her the truth. She was petrified. I told her I fucking loved her, and she still left. End of story."

"No, something's not right here," Lilly says. "She loves you. It makes little sense. And if you loved her like you say you do, you wouldn't be sitting here drowning your sorrows. You'd be out looking for her because you and I both fucking know the safest place for her is here!" Rising from her seat, Lilly scoffs, "See you later, boys. Sit here and cry in your fucking drinks. I'm gonna go do what needs to be done and find her." With that parting shot, she gets up and walks out of the bar.

Matt leans forward and rakes his hands through his hair. "What have I done?" He looks to Jax, then turns his head away. "I love her. I fucking worship her."

Jax sighs. "We knew it could happen, Matt. We're the bogeyman to some, and to others the Homani never existed."

Matt glances over at Jax. "You didn't see her fear. She couldn't wait to get away from me fast enough."

Jax claps Matt on the back. "You love her, buddy. Go find her, talk to her; Calli will come around. She loves you, too. She's your mate. You need her."

Matt stares at Jax. "I didn't even get to explain that. Everything happened so fast that I let my temper get the better of me. I just walked out the door. I didn't explain everything."

"Then go. Find Calli and explain everything. If she doesn't love you like, I think she loves you, then there's no hope for any of us."

Matt grins at his longtime friend, "Thanks, man. I got a woman to track down." Matt says as he leaves the bar.

"Go get her, tiger!" Jax yells out.

Matt turns with a smirk. "That would be you, not me. I'm a fucking wolf," he says as he stalks out the door. He hears the echo of Jax's laugh as he jumps in his truck.

CALLI STANDS ON THE SIDEWALK, looking toward the town she can't bring herself to walk through, knowing what she knows. Looking into the woods to the right, she decides to take the back trails to the gate to avoid running into anyone.

Darkness has fallen, but a full moon and clear sky give just enough light for Calli to see her way. Heartbroken, with tears streaming down her face, Calli sets out upon the first path knowing if she stays due east, she should come out to the road by the gate.

The Homani, she thinks in wonder. The joy filling her in knowing that they are alive and well is overwhelming. Her fear of the repercussions of being with them immediately follows this thought, keeping her at a steady pace.

Her mother's voice echoes in her head. *Never let them find you, Calli. They won't understand. It'll be a death sentence.*

Lost in her thoughts, the sound of a deep growl brings Calli to an abrupt halt.

Cautiously looking around, Calli tries to peer through the trees to see what made that sound. A twig snaps to her left, and Calli whips around, seeing nothing but shadows. The fine hairs on her arms prickle with the feeling of being hunted. She knows there are no wild animals in these woods as they belong to the Homani, and they are the Apex predators.

Whatever is out there, it has to be Homani. Fear rises from the core of her belly. Calli takes off at a fast run, branches and thorns tearing at her skin and clothing. The sound of heavy pads crushing the ground gets closer to her.

"Drop, Calli!" Lilly yells as she leaps into the air, morphing into a panther and landing with a heavy thud.

Covering her mouth with both hands to keep from screaming, Calli is in shock after witnessing a Homani change.

The Lilly-Panther quietly stalks a few feet into the woods and lets out a deafening roar echoing through the trees. Her long, sleek black fur glimmers in the moonlight.

Tail twitching in an aggravated manner, the panther glances back at Calli, then stares intensely into the woods.

She's protecting me. Holy shit, Calli stares in awe as the panther stands guard. Minutes that feel like hours pass before the Lily-panther turns in Calli's direction and strolls towards her. Stopping only a few feet away, Lilly changes to her human form. Her tattered clothes are strewn about the forest grounds. Comfortable in her nudity, Lily approaches Calli. "Are you okay?"

"I am, I am," Calli stutters in shock, averting her eyes from Lily's well-toned naked body.

Lilly kneels down to where Calli is sitting on the ground. "Are you hurt?"

"I think I'm just in shock." Calli answers. Lilly smiles, her bright turquoise eyes shining as she holds her hand out to her.

"Hi, I'm Lilly, and I'm a Homani panther. Nice to meet you," she chuckles.

Taking Lilly's hand in hers as she's helped off the ground, Calli gives her a wide smile. "I'm Calli, human. Nice to meet you," she replies, and they laugh at the absurdity. Calli glances back at the woods, "Who or what was that?" she inquires as she removes her jacket and hands it to Lilly.

"I'm not sure who it was, Calli. I didn't pick up their scent. I could probably go back and track them, but I don't wanna leave you alone," Lilly says as she once again scans the surrounding forest.

Calli and Lilly work their way back through the trail toward the main house as Matt's truck comes to a screeching halt. He jumps out and rushes to Calli and Lilly, seeing her torn clothing and scrapes.

"I was looking for you everywhere. I couldn't find you anywhere in town. Are you okay?" Matt asks as his hands open and close like he wants to touch her. Worry and fear are evident on his face. Taking a step forward, Matt seems relieved when Calli doesn't flinch away from him. Slowly approaching her, he cautiously reaches out to inspect her wounds.

"I'm okay, Matt," Calli murmurs, comforted by his touch.

Encouraged by her reaction, Matt gathers Calli in his arms. "I thought I lost you." Matt's voice breaks with emotion.

It overwhelms Calli with her love for Matt. *I can't leave him,* she thinks. *This is where I belong.*

Her mother's voice tries to invade her mind, but she shuts her thoughts down. *I won't let the past dictate my future.* A rightness and peace settle over Calli. Wrapping her arms around his neck, she gazes into Matt's eyes. "I'm so sorry. I was foolish to run."

A throat clearing reminds them they have an audience. Not wanting to let go, Matt turns to Lilly with Calli still in his arms. "What happened out there?" He gestures to the woods with his chin.

"It seemed like she was being hunted. I had to shift in front of her, Matt. I'm sorry," Lilly says, looking down uncomfortably at the ground.

"Why would you apologize?" Calli says, rushing to Lilly's defense. "You saved my life!"

Glaring at Lilly, Matt replies, "We have strict rules here, Calli. Rule number one is to never shift in front of a non-Homani unless they are your mate or the mate of another Homani."

Lilly perks up at Matt's comment. "Then I guess I didn't break any rules. You two have a good night. Matt, we'll talk about who could be stalking Calli tomorrow," she says with a shit-eating grin as she strides away.

"Mate?" Calli questions, looking at Matt, confused.

Matt guides Calli to the truck by giving her a quick kiss on the top of her head and a light squeeze. "Come on. We need to get you cleaned up," he answers, avoiding her question.

When they arrive at the house, Matt scoops Calli in his arms and carries her to the bathroom, where he gently sits her on the vanity chair.

Turning to run a bath for her, he adds some Epsom salts and lavender oil to soothe her muscles. Watching him from her perch, Calli marvels at how fortunate she is to have such a wonderful man who loves her.

Helping her undress, Matt eases Calli into the tub. As he is about to remove his shirt, he pauses, waiting for permission to join her. Noticing his dilemma, Calli reaches out to help him undress.

"You never have to fear me, Calli," Matt explains with love in his eyes. "I would destroy what's left of this world for you," he says with conviction as he slides in behind her. Snuggling in his arms, Calli kisses his muscled biceps. "I love you, Matt."

Pulling back her hair to turn her face towards him, Matt leans in, their lips barely touching. "I love you, Calli," he growls before crashing his mouth to hers, their tongues entwining in an ancient dance of desire.

ELEVEN

Calli awakes, stretching her aching muscles from their lovemaking the night before. She turns to the man lying beside her with a small smile. His face is so peaceful in sleep, his long lashes dark against his tan skin, full lips slightly parted in slumber.

Not wanting to wake him, Calli slowly rises from the bed, letting out a squeal when a solid muscular arm surrounds her waist and hauls her back against a broad chest.

"Where are you going, little hellcat?" he growls in her ear, biting the lobe.

"Why, to make you breakfast, boss?" She bats her eyelashes.

Rolling over on top of her and pinning her to the bed, Matt lightly pinches her nipple between his teeth. "Not before I make breakfast of you," he says with a wicked gleam in his eye as he works light kisses down her body.

Goosebumps rise on Calli's skin as Matt's mouth worships his way to her inner thigh, nipping along the outside of her mound. Calli threads her hands into Matt's hair with a moan, pulling his face to her sweet spot. Then she lets out a frustrated groan when he slips his mouth to her other thigh, teasing her. "Patience, Kitten," he chuckles.

"Matt!" Calli squeals when he licks her from slit to clit, sucking the nub into his mouth. Calli's back arches off the bed as her orgasm builds, her body tight as a bow with its imminent release. Feasting on her, Matt holds her thighs wide with his steel grip, savouring her every twitch and pulse. Matt hums his satisfaction, lapping up her juices as she explodes in his mouth.

Crawling back up to hold her in his arms as she recovers, Matt quips, "Breakfast, the most important meal of the day."

Calli giggles and kisses him lovingly. Snuggling close, she lets out a long sigh. With a light kiss on her shoulder, Matt inquires, "What's on your mind?"

"Well, you know I appreciate working for you, but to be honest, there's not a lot to do," she states hesitantly. "Would you mind if I helped around town? Someone must need an extra set of hands."

Giving her shoulder a light bite, Matt chuckles. "I'm sure someone does. Speak to the shop owners and maybe check out down by the fields. I'll get the word out when I'm doing my rounds today. But Calli, take Jax with you. We still don't know who was in the woods yesterday. With Lilly having the shop to run, she wouldn't be able to guard you. So I can have someone else take over Jax's duties for now."

Calli kisses Matt slowly, turning to face him. "I don't like the idea of having a bodyguard," she pauses as Matt's low growl rumbles in his chest, "but if it keeps your beastie at bay, I will."

After tidying the house, Calli hops into the shower, excited about the prospect of a job. Taking extra care with her long auburn locks, she eventually grabs a cowboy hat and shoves it on her head in defeat. Humidity is clearly winning the hair battle. With her tank top, jeans, and shit-kicker boots, she admires the badass looking back at her in the mirror.

"You've got this," Calli reassures her reflection.

The sound of a truck pulling up front has Calli dashing out the door. Grinning wide as she hops in the truck's cab. "Morning, Jax!" she says to the man who will be her escort for the day.

With a cheeky grin, Jax winks. "Morning, beautiful. You ready to be unleashed on the locals?"

"You know it!" Calli lets out a whoop. Laughing, Jax puts the truck in gear and turns them toward town.

The walkie-talkie on Jax's hip crackles to life. "You got my girl with you?" Matt's voice comes over the radio.

Rolling his eyes at Calli, "Yes, Matt. We're on our way now. Going to give the lady a tour and history lesson of the town before she decides on her first stop."

"Keep your eyes on the road and off her, Jax," Matt growls, "over and out."

Throwing his head back with a howl, Jax laughs. "Oh, he's got it bad."

Calli, embarrassed by Matt's warning, blushes. Seeing her reaction, Jax turns serious. "Any male worth his salt would die for his mate. We're a protective lot, Calli."

Turning to face Jax, Calli asks, "That's the second time I've heard that word, mate. Is that like a boyfriend?"

"Wow, okay. This should be a conversation for Matt, but I know communication isn't his thing. Dictating, now that's another story. I'll start at the beginning, Homani history 101," he says as he turns toward the outskirts of town.

With a faraway look in his eyes, Jax begins. "By the time the special-ops stormed the blackout sites where we were being held, the scientists had succeeded in their experiment. We were faster and stronger, and our intelligence was off the charts. Sense of smell, hearing and eyesight all increased. Our hunting and fighting skills were developing. We were being trained. We could shift into whatever animal was predominant in our DNA. The nanobots had merged us as one. The scientists didn't realize the other traits we had picked up, ones they hadn't intended. Lions, tigers, bears, and wolves don't mate for life, and neither do most humans, for that matter, but something happened in our chemical makeup. Not only could we smell our mate when we met them, but we also mate for life."

Jax pauses, his hand griping the steering wheel. He glances out the driver's side window, avoiding Calli's gaze. "I've seen what happens to a mated pair if they're separated," his voice is barely a whisper. "They die Calli. Well, if they're both Homani, they do. If one is human, the human may survive. They just wish they didn't." His words slamming into her as if he'd screamed them.

Calli's hand flies to her mouth as if to hold in the horror she feels at what Jax had just told her, could be shoved back down and denied. She takes a few deep breaths to calm herself. "Are you saying that I'm Matt's mate and if I leave or something happens to me, he dies?" she asks, her voice cracking.

"Yes." Jax says simply.

"Why wouldn't Matt tell me, Jax?" Calli cries.

Frustrated, Jax replies, "I don't know, Calli. If I were to guess? If it were me? To protect you."

"Protect me?" Calli interrupts Jax. "Protect me from what?"

Jax hits the brakes, and the truck lurches forward. He swings his arm out to stop Calli from hitting the dash. A quick glance tells him she is okay. Turning towards her in the seat, his eyes flash briefly, a sure sign of his current anger.

"Yes, damn it! To protect you! To let you make your choice of whether you want to accept the love that is being offered. Not having a feeling of obligation because a fucking life would be on the line. That's true love, Calli. Sometimes we keep things to ourselves to protect those we love. Would you ever want to question if your soul mate was with you because they felt the same or because they felt they had to? That's the real fucking Homani curse!" Jax deflates, slumping in his seat, his anger leaving him. Sadness takes its place.

Calli sits quietly in the truck, tears slowly rolling down her face. "I, I left," she whispers. "Jax, I left. Matt could have died! Holy fuck, Jax! When I left, we could've both died!"

Jax looks over at Cali and says quietly, "Yeah, he could have Calli, but he would have died for you if you wanted to go. He'd never stop you. We would've gone after you, keeping you close enough for your safety."

Anger taking the place of horror, Calli turns to Jax. "I don't know if I want to hug Matt or hit him! I'm so fucking mad! I love him, Jax. I would never want him to doubt that. You said that humans didn't always die, but wish they did. What happened?" she asks.

"Well," Jax replies, "once the ops team rescued us from a blackout site in Washington, the state where we were being held, we walked up here to Northern British Columbia. There were some humans with us. Some people on the inside had helped them with Intel so we could escape. Some of these humans had formed mate bonds with some of the older Homani. Not everybody made the trek. It was long and hard, and people were hunting us. One of the older Homani had shifted to protect his mate, and they shot him. We had to keep going. They had to knock out his mate because she wanted to stay with his body. She just started to whither away. It was like she had lost her will to live. She died when that bullet pierced his heart, just as surely as if it had pierced hers. It didn't happen all at once, but within six months she was a shell of her former self. She would hardly eat and she could barely keep it down when she did. We had to force her to take water. She was a walking corpse. Eventually, she just didn't wake up one morning. We believe she died of a broken heart. It was one of the saddest things I had ever witnessed. Over the years, we realized if we separated mates for too long a time, they both seemed to suffer the same consequences. It's almost like their bodies can't function if their mate isn't near them. They break down physically and shut down mentally."

To absorb all of what Jax had just said, Calli sat quietly—amazed at the Homani's resilience. They suffered experiments and then the arduous trek to Northern Canada. They were building a new home for themselves. Calli's respect and admiration grew exponentially.

"How many were there?" Calli asks.

"I was only about ten or twelve at the time, but I think there were eight hundred of us in total. That included the humans and the rescue team. So only about six hundred of us made it here. We were lucky, though. Harold Cooter and Peter Johnson had been monitoring and working in the dam when the bombs dropped. Most of the workers had run, trying to get home to their families. Harold and Peter? They stayed behind. Harold was ex-special ops and a friend of somebody on the team that rescued us. They had a plan all along for us to come this way. Since Peter knew the area, he'd been scavenging for supplies and getting some things ready so that we'd have some sort of tent city when we arrived. Over time, some people trained as security details, and others started opening little tent shops. Eventually, it became what you see now. Since most of us never had a last name, we chose Smith. It was a fresh start for all of us, we chose Smith because it was generic and we didn't want to stand out. Hence, Smith Farms. We had always heard rumours that the Homani didn't survive, Harold and Peter, they fueled those rumours to keep our secret."

Jax gives Calli a playful shove on the shoulder. Then he says, "Enough of the dark history lesson. Let's find you a job here other than catering to Matt." He wiggles eyebrows jokingly. "Where do you want to start?"

Appreciating Jax's trying to lighten the situation, Calli smiles and says, "You know what? Since the town depends on food so much, let's try farming."

"Show me what you got, girl!" Jax turns the truck toward the vast fields.

CHAPTER

TWELVE

The bright red barns loom in the distance. As they pull up in front of the first barn, Calli notices a gorgeous, petite brunette coming out of the barn, striding towards the truck. A tiny spitfire with a fuck around and find out grin. Following Jax's lead of hopping out of the truck, Calli walks around and waits for introductions.

"Hey, Kate," Jax greets her. Appraising the fields, he says, "It's going to be harvest time soon by the looks of things."

Kate follows Jax's gaze. "Yeah, it's a good bumper crop this year. The weather's been suitable for it. " She glances over at Calli, her gaze questioning.

"Kate, this is Matt's mate, Calli. Calli, this is Kate, the head foreman here."

Shaking each other's hands, Kate says, "A pleasure to meet you, Calli. It's about damn time Matt got himself a mate."

Standing back, she looks Calli up and down. "And a damn fine one at that. Good for him. I heard rumours, but you know what it's like here. You fart at one end of town, and by the time you get to the other side, you've shit yourself." She cackles at her joke.

"Now that about sums up living with small-town gossip perfectly," Jax laughs with Kate.

Surveying the fields, barns and animals that she can see, Calli's gaze zeros in on a rustic tractor parked next to the barn. "Does that run?" she asks, looking at Kate.

Kate smirks. "Old Bessie? Yeah, she runs fine. Want to give her a go?"

"Uh, Calli, do you know how to drive?" Jax asks cautiously.

"Well, not really, but I figured that," she says, pointing to the rustic tractor, "would be a safe place to start."

"She's not wrong, Jax," Kate replies. "It's a wide-open field. How much harm could she cause?"

Excited, Calli runs up to the tractor, glancing at Kate for reassurance as she climbs into the seat. Kate steps forward, pointing at the controls in a brief tutorial. Seemingly confident in Calli's understanding, Kate jumps down and moves out of the way. Jax and Kate watch as Calli brings Bessie to life, turning her towards the open field.

After a few practice runs, her confidence building, she steers the tractor towards the barn where Kate and Jax are waiting.

Calli's foot catches on the clutch as the tractor lumbers closer, popping it and causing it to lurch forward. Jax, noticing Callis's distress, jumps on to help. In a panic, Calli jerks the wheel at the last minute, almost clipping Jax. However, his superhuman reflexes save him from being trampled by Old Bessie. Kate leaps up on the back of the tractor, bringing it to an abrupt halt.

Shaking, Calli jumps off the tractor. Jax, still on the

ground, slowly rises to his feet. "Maybe that's enough of a driving lesson for today," he says as he dusts off his jeans.

Kate walks up to them and pats Calli on the back. "Not bad for your first time, but I agree with Jax. I think that's enough for today."

When she and Jax's are both safely in the trucks cab, Calli slumps in defeat and lets out a sigh. "Well, that was a bust. Sorry, I almost ran over you."

"Hey, you were doing great. Bessie's temperamental. Maybe we should have started you out on the side-by-sides," Jax replies, trying to cheer her up.

Turning towards town, they sit in silence. Calli licks the wounds from her bruised ego, while Jax contemplates where to take her next. After a while, Jax pulls up in front of the local watering hole, Dusk till Dawn.

"Kinda early for a drink, don't you think?" Calli asks, glancing at the bar out her window.

Pointing out a few cars in the parking lot, Jax raises his eyebrows at Calli. "Well, for some, it's obviously five o'clock somewhere."

The smell of stale beer and wood polish hit Calli first as her eyes adjust to the dimness of the bar's interior. Stools line the long oak top, a few currently occupied by some regulars. A few turn to greet Jax as they make their way to the bar.

A tall, stunning blonde is polishing glasses near the end. A megawatt smile lights her face as she notices Jax and Calli. "Hey Jax, a bit early for you. What can I do for you?" She gives him a flirty wink.

"Actually, Dawn, I wanted to introduce you to Matt's mate, Calli." He gestures to Calli, grinning.

Reaching out to shake Dawn's hand, her grip firm, Dawn cocks her head to the side to size her up.

"Matt's mate," she repeats. "I'd heard the rumor. So glad to finally meet you in person, Calli," she finishes with a curt nod, giving her approval.

"Matt's been keeping her to himself. So it's high time she got out to meet the locals. Calli's also looking to help around town," Jax tells her.

Laughing, Dawn lines up a few glasses in front of her as she prepares drinks. "I could always use an extra hand. You ever bartended before, Calli?"

She glances nervously at Jax, wide-eyed. "Uh, no, but I'm willing to learn." Calli straightens her shoulders with determination. With a nod, Dawn motions to Calli behind the bar. Dawn begins her quick tutorial by pulling down bottles from the shelf on the wall behind the bar.

"Here are your main men. Calli, meet Jack, Jim, Johnny, Jameson and Jose. All the J's." She extends her arm, palms up, as if introducing a particular group.

Staring at the bottles like the foreign entities they are to her, Calli reaches out to the first one. Bringing it to her nose, she takes a light whiff. Her face immediately screws up as she recoils. "People drink this stuff?" she asks.

Dawn's jaw drops. "Have you never had a drink, Calli?"

Biting her lip, Calli looks warily at the bottles lined up in front of her. "Uh, not really. I snuck a sip of beer once when I was a teenager," she says, looking embarrassed at her inexperience.

Clapping her hands together with a mischievous sparkle in her eyes, Dawn lines up five shot glasses and pours half shots in each.

Reaching for the bottle, Jax tries to stop Dawn, "Uh. I don't think that's a good idea."

"She'll be fine. They're just half-shots. She needs to know the flavors if she's going to mix a drink."

Calli nods in agreement, "Really, Jax, Dawn's right. What could it hurt?"

Standing back to watch the shit show that is about to unfold, Jax waits as Calli brings the first shot to her lips.

"Bottoms up!" Dawn yells, and the bar patrons cheer.

A bitter taste hits Calli's tongue first as a slow burn slides down her throat, stealing her breath. Coughing and wheezing, she immediately grabs for the second shot, thinking she should get this over with quickly if she is to survive.

Jax lurches forward to stop her.

"Slow down, Calli. That will hit you hard. Matt will kill me if I have to carry you home!"

With the fourth shot already giving her a pleasant tingling feeling, Calli sidesteps Jax and downs the fifth, grinning from ear to ear. "I did it!" she exclaims, giving Dawn a high-five, her aim a little off.

Dawn and Calli discuss the various drink recipes as Calli takes notes. Once Dawn feels Calli has a decent grasp of the basics, she lets Calli loose on the patrons, mixing their drink orders.

Jax takes a seat in the corner where he can observe and is soon joined by Harold and Peter to discuss the retrofit for the dam.

A burst of raucous laughter has the men at the table looking up just in time to see Calli light a drink called flaming sambuca. Unfortunately, her coordination is off from consuming the many drinks the customers had been buying her.

Calli lights the glass but knocks it over in her haste to celebrate. The flaming alcohol trails down the length of the bar like a firewall, causing the partygoers to jump back and Dawn to grab a bag of salt to extinguish the flames. With a yelp, Calli jumps back, stumbling into the counter behind her.

Jax is there in an instant. "Are you okay?"

Swaying slightly, Calli giggles, "It went poof!" she slurs.

Noticing her flushed face and glassy eyes, Jax realizes Calli is drunk.

"Oh fuck, Matt's going to kill me! How many drinks did you have?" he asks.

"Dunno. They kept buying me shots; I didn't want to be rude and not drink them," she whines.

Overhearing Calli, Dawn bursts out laughing, "Oh good lord Calli, there's a trick to that. We have a spit bottle under the counter. Just turn away, pretend you're chasing it with a beer and discreetly spit the shot back out," she finishes, bent over, laughing.

"Shit Dawn, get her some coffee. If Matt shows up and sees her like this, we're both going to deal with his wolf!"

Scrambling over to the coffee pot, Dawn pours a sizeable black coffee as Jax sits Calli down at a nearby table.

"Here, drink." Dawn pushes the steaming brew in front of Calli.

Gulping down the coffee, Calli leans back in the chair. After a moment, her mouth waters, thick with saliva. Then, looking around in a panic, Calli leans to the side and vomits her coffee on the floor.

Quickly reaching out to hold back her hair, Jax rubs her back with his other hand as Dawn runs to get Calli a glass of water and a mop for the still-steaming coffee that has made a reappearance.

Dawn glances at Jax, handing the water to Calli, saying, "We're fucked."

Jax only nods in agreement. The resignation on his face over his impending doom mirrored Dawn's.

The radio on his hip crackles to life, startling Jax. "Jax, it's Pete. Could you swing by Brook's hardware and grab that transistor for me? She said it should be in today."

Grateful that it wasn't Matt and a reason to delay bringing Calli home, Jax immediately answers, "Not a problem, Pete. I'll have it out to you in thirty. Over and out."

Helping Calli out of the bar and into the truck's cab, Jax takes his time driving through the main street. Then, pulling in front of the hardware store, Jax regards Calli, giving her a once over and gauging her sobriety level.

"You good here if I run in and grab a part for Pete? We'll take it out to him at the dam. It'll give you a chance to see it firsthand."

Calli sips the canteen of water Dawn gave her and nods her assent. Satisfied, Jax walks into the shop.

CALLI WIPES HER MOUTH, jerking awake, realizing she had nodded off to sleep. She slowly gets out of the truck with a bladder about to burst. Looking up and down the street, she settles on the hardware store, hoping they have a washroom she can use.

The bell above the door announces her presence. Glancing around, hopping from one foot to the other, Calli was desperate to either find Jax or an employee before she pees right there on the floor.

A beautiful, bespectacled redhead with a heart-shaped face and intelligent eyes approaches Calli. "Can I help you?"

Dancing from one foot to the other, Calli urgently asks, "Do you have a washroom I could use?"

Seeing the urgency of the matter, the redhead leads Calli to the back so that she can relieve herself.

"All good?" she asks when Calli emerges from the bathroom.

"Yes, thank you." Calli sticks out her hand. "I'm Calli, Matt's mate," she says.

Shaking her hand, the redhead smiles and introduces herself. "I'm Brook, and this," she gestures around, "is my store. If there's anything I can help you with, let me know. It was a pleasure meeting you." With that she wanders back to the front of the store, leaving Calli on her own to explore.

Walking the aisles looking for Jax, Calli scans the shelves as she goes. Spying a rope reel, a blush heats Calli's cheeks, remembering Matt tying her up with his belt the night before.

Wanting to add to their collection of makeshift toys, Calli glances around, looking for Brook. Shrugging, Calli acquires the rope herself. Pulling on the end, trying to gauge how much she'll need, the well-oiled reel spins much faster than expected. Reaching out to stop it, Calli's foot catches in the tangled mess on the floor, causing her to lose her balance and fall onto the shelf behind her. Tipping precariously, the shelf topples over, causing Calli to land spread-eagle on the floor at its base.

A crash and yelp from the other side have Calli sitting up in alarm.

A paint-splattered Jax storms around the corner as Brook appears from the opposite end. Glancing at Calli on the floor and Jax's thunderous expression as paint drips down his brow, Brook doubles over with laughter.

"Calli! What the fuck?" Jax growls, "I thought you were staying in the truck!"

"Oh, Jax, calm your claws. Can't you see the poor girl is mortified?" Gasping for breath through her laughter, Brook hands him her apron to clean himself. "Found the paint colour you were looking for?" She smirks, raising an eyebrow before her giggles overtake her again.

Jax glares at Brook, wiping his face. "Yeah, I'm wearing it. Have fun cleaning up the mess on aisle three." Then, tossing the paint-filled apron on the floor, he reaches out to help Calli up. "Come on, trouble. Let's get you sober."

Checking Calli over for any signs of injury, Jax informs Brook, "I'll be back to get that transistor later." Glancing down at his paint-filled clothes he adds, "After I clean up."

Ducking her head, Calli gives Brook a slight wave and follows Jax out the door.

Unclipping his walkie-talkie from his belt, Jax wipes the paint off of it, giving Calli a humorous look. "Matt, it's Jax. I'm dropping Calli off at the diner. I'll make sure April keeps an eye on her. Uh, something's come up that I need to take care of."

The sound of Matt's voice crackles over the speaker. "What could be more important than guarding my mate, Jax?" he says, deceptively quiet.

Squirming in his seat as if Matt were glaring at him in person, Jax casts a quick glance at Calli. "Well, uh, you see, there was a bit of a mishap at the hardware store. Calli's fine!" he says in a rush to reassure Matt. "I, uh, just need to run home and change."

Matt's low growl could be clearly heard over the mic. "Put Calli on, now, Jax!"

Jax hands Calli the receiver with a pleading look in his eyes. "Hey Matt," Calli chirps a little too cheerily, "Having a great day with Jax, heading into the diner now, love yoooooooooouu-uuuu!" she drawls out the last in a long singsong voice.

Snatching the receiver back from her, Jax looks to the heavens, praying for a quick death. "See, all good here, Matt. Just giving you an update. Gotta run. Over and out!" he rushes out and clicks off the walkie-talkie.

"Come on, let's get some coffee and food into you before Matt arrives," Jax says as he climbs out of the truck.

THE SMELL of freshly baked goods consumes Calli's senses as she walks through the diner doors. A throwback to the nineteen fifties, the long counter with red leather stools lines the front with a display showcasing freshly baked pastries. Calli recalls seeing a similar scene in an old magazine she had once found long ago. Tables line the walls with booths for family or friends to enjoy their meals together.

Since it was only mid-afternoon, the diner had only a few customers. A motherly blonde with kind blue eyes is wiping down the counter as she trades barbs with the locals seated there.

Not missing a beat, she looks up and greets Jax with a broad smile and a quick hello. Steering Calli to a seat at the end, Jax waves her over.

"April, this is Calli, Matt's mate."

Wiping her hands on her apron, April then extends her hand. "Pleasure to meet the woman who finally stole Matt's heart," she greets Calli warmly.

Slightly blushing, Calli smiles and shakes her hand.

April glances back nervously at the kitchen doors. "The menu's a little limited today. Maverick didn't show up for his shift. He's my cook three days a week," she informs Calli.

Narrowing his eyes, Jax seems lost in thought before replying, "That's fine, just a black coffee and a sandwich for Calli. I need to get cleaned up," he says ruefully, looking down at his paint-splattered clothing.

"I was going to ask," she gestures at him, waving her hand up and down, chuckling.

Calli covers her face with her hands. "It's my fault," she groans.

Laughing, April pours Calli a coffee, then starts preparing a sandwich. "I'm sure there's a good story there," she begins when a group of diners walk in, "but it looks like the dinner crowd is early."

She places the sandwich in front of Calli, patting her hand before she moves on to the new customers.

Jax turns to leave, catching April's eye. "Monitor her until Matt arrives."

With a quick nod, April hurries to fill the orders coming from the customers.

With her belly full, Calli watches as April touches each table, taking their orders and laughing at one conversation or the next. As more people arrive, Calli notices the tight lines of stress forming around April's eyes, though her smile never reveals how overwhelmed she is.

Leaving her stool, Calli wanders into the kitchen. In a

large stockpot, they had set a chicken to boil. Biscuit dough is rising on a rack in the corner.

Opening the cupboard and the walk-in refrigerator, Calli forms a plan. Putting the old recipe books she had used to teach herself to read to good use, she quickly debones the chicken and chops up some vegetables. She places the biscuits in the oven and gets to work using sour cream, butter, and chicken broth. Twenty minutes later, Calli is scooping out her version of chicken pot pie with a freshly baked biscuit on top.

Barreling through the kitchen door, April stops in her tracks. "Oh, my god! You're a lifesaver!" Turning on her heel, she yells out to the diners, "Change of plans. Sandwiches are off the menu. So instead, we have the Calli special, chicken pot pie!"

A cheer went up in the crowd. April rushes over and gives Calli a quick hug. "When can you start?"

"Are you serious?" Calli asks excitedly.

"Dead serious, you just saved me from a riot out there," April grins.

Grabbing a platter of food, Calli walks around April. "No time like the present," she quips as she strolls out to help serve the customers.

April and Calli are clearing down the kitchen when Matt arrives. By this time, the diners have all been fed and given glowing reviews of Calli's meal.

Elated, Calli rushes up to Matt as he scoops her in his arms, his mouth descending on hers in a passionate kiss. "How's my girl?" he asks when they finally come up for air.

Watching from the side with a satisfied smile, April answers, "Your girl was a godsend. I see now why you've been keeping her to yourself."

"Matt! April offered me a job!" She beams up at him.

"That's great, Calli!" he says, giving her another squeeze. Kissing the top of her head, he glances over at April and gives her a nod of thanks.

April hands Matt a wrapped dish. "That girl can cook."

Taking the plate in one hand with his arm still around Calli, they leave the diner.

THIRTEEN

As the days pass, Calli enjoys her new job at the diner. The locals treat her as one of them; it gives her hope that she is becoming an accepted part of the community. However, with harvesting season upon them, Matt has been working long days, leaving Calli to spend more time with Lilly.

"You ready?" Lilly's head pops around the corner of Calli's bathroom door, where she is attempting to tame her long tresses.

"Almost done." She replies, giving herself one last check in the mirror.

She and Lilly have a girls' night out at Dusk til Dawn's. The boys are working late up at the dam, trying to retrofit the new transistor.

Calli glances in the mirror once more. Using charcoal, her smokey eye makeup gives her emerald eyes a luminous glow. Having tied her hair with strips of cloth the night before, her long auburn locks are curled in spirals down her back. A black corset top highlights her full breasts and is comfortable around her waist. With her black jeans and shit-kicker boots, she looks stunning.

A whistle from the doorway has Calli turning with a grin. "Too much?"

"Fuck no! Matt will not know what hit him when he joins us later. Don't be surprised if he hauls you out to the bar and rails you over the truck's cab." Lilly laughs with a knowing grin. "On second thought, he may kill any man who looks your way, too," shrugging. "either way, there will be some excitement tonight."

"Lilly!"

"Just calling it as I see it. So let's get this show on the road."

Walking out into the night air, the crisp, incredible fragrance of fall envelopes them. With the sun setting to the west, the sky is alight with orange, pink, and red hues. The leaves, just falling, are vibrant with their colors. Calli inhales a deep breath. "I love that smell. Earthy, with a woodsy undertone." Lilly nods her agreement.

Passing the shops through town as they make their way to the bar, a low, rumbling growl from the alleyway has them pausing. Clasping Calli's arm, Lilly's firm grip warns her not to move. Tilting her head slowly left and right, her eyes flashing turquoise, Calli knows that Lilly's panther is close to the surface. With a slight jerk on her arm, Lilly urges Calli forward towards the bar.

"What the hell was that?" Calli looks at Lilly, trying to keep up with her rapid pace.

"I'm not sure. We've had no incidents since the woods, but I'm not taking any chances." Lilly tries to reassure her friend.

PULLING BACK IN THE SHADOWS, watching the two women hurry down the street, the homani stifles the growl that is clawing up his throat. *Fucking cunt. You may have them fooled, but I know who you are. Secrets, secrets, you have many little girl. Your long red hair is a fitting testament to the spilled blood that is your legacy. YOU WILL PAY! I'm a patient man. Your kind has trained me well. I will have my pound of flesh.*

THE BAND IS JUST STARTING their first set on stage when Calli and Lilly walk into the bar.

A few of the younger locals cover whatever genre of music they can get their hands on. Brook is a tremendous asset for acquiring records from when music was plentiful. Her collection is the envy of most people. Tonight could be a mix of rock, pop, and country, with a smattering of reggae. No one cares. The music is pleasant, and the dance floor will be packed.

With the place filling fast, Lilly grabs Calli's arm and muscles her way to a table near the stage. "Yes! We scored great seats," she fist-bumps Calli before she drops her jacket on the back of her chair.

"Did you want to grab the first round while I use the ladies' room?"

Glancing at the bar, Calli notices Dawn is working with another young bartender. "Sure, what would you like?"

"Anything but a flaming sambuca!" Lilly replies with a comical look before bursting into laughter.

Calli rolls her eyes. "You set one bar top on fire one time, and you never live it down," she quips, strolling towards the bar.

"What can I get my favorite apprentice?" Dawn leans towards Calli, giving her a cheeky grin and a wink.

She laughs. "I think my bartending days are over, thanks. The diner is definitely more my speed. Can I get a martini for Lilly, and I'll have a light beer, please?"

Dawn swings around, wrapping her knuckles on the bar. "Coming right up!"

Placing her drinks in front of Calli, Dawn's nose twitches. "Cookies!"

Calli looks at her in confusion.

"Don't hold out on me, Calli. I know you have homemade chocolate chip cookies on you somewhere," she exclaims, tapping her nose.

Reaching into the inside pocket of her jacket, Calli produces two neatly wrapped cookies and hands them to Dawn. "These were for Matt, but we'll keep this our secret." She winks as she gives Dawn the cookies.

"The Homani senses never cease to amaze me." Calli chuckles.

Drinks in hand, Calli weaves her way through the crowd, finally arriving at their table. Lilly reaches for hers, then clinks it to Calli's beer.

"Cheers! To a night of drinking, dancing and shenanigans!" Then, grabbing her arm, she drags Calli out onto the dance floor.

Calli raises her beer to her lips, letting the cold brew soothe her already overheated body as she slumps back in her seat. The stamina of the Homani was impressive. She could attest to that after spending many nights in Matt's arms. Finally, she gives up on the dance floor and trying to keep pace with Lilly.

A commotion at the front of the bar has Calli raising her head, and a crash and the sound of breaking glass has her on her feet. A loud howl cuts through the air, followed by a deep growl. Covering her ears Calli's eyes search for Lilly.

Standing on the chair for a better view, Calli's eyes widen when she sees the enormous blonde wolf destroying the front of the bar. Three burly men are trying to distract the wolf as another group pushes back the crowd.

Having only seen Lilly's panther and only once, that night in the woods, Calli is frozen in place by the sheer size of the wolf that is now trying to snap and bite the surrounding men.

Suddenly, a familiar voice bellows from the front door, "Dawn! Change back, now!" Dawn's wolf lowers her head, teeth barred with the hair rising along her spine.

"I don't want to hurt you!" he growls his stern warning.

Calli's heart was in her throat, "Oh my god, no! Matt!"

Jumping off the chair to rush to his side, Calli comes to a stop when two steel bands wrap around her from behind. "No, Calli." Jax holds firm. "Matt will be okay. This is his to handle."

Helpless to do anything but watch, Calli searches out Matt once again. He's slowly circling Dawn, palms out in a placating manner.

In her wolf form, she comes to waist level with Matt.

Calli can hear his low tones across the bar. No doubt the

Homani understood his words, but as her hearing is on the human level, whatever he's saying is lost to her.

Leaning down to her ear, Jax repeats what Matt is saying for Calli. "He's calming her, trying to get her to change back. She's fighting him, not a challenge, but either refusing or she can't follow his orders." The concern is apparent in his voice.

A rumble flows through the crowd, then suddenly, an enormous black wolf lunges, pinning Dawn in wolf form down on the bar top. The creak and groaning of wood give a split-second warning before it crumbles under their weight.

Not losing his grip, the black wolf drags a thrashing Dawn out of the bar and away from the crowd.

Relaxing his hold on Calli as Lilly approaches, Jax raises his chin to where the commotion occurred. "What the fuck, Lilly? I haven't seen Dawn lose control like that since the cages."

"Neither have I," she murmurs, biting her lip with a far away look.

Calli stands motionless, her face pale. Finally, she clears her throat. "Should we check on Matt?"

Jax and Lilly turn towards her. "Yeah, I'll go. Lilly, it should be safe out there," he motions toward the exit, "can you get this crowd out? Matt and I will question Dawn. Touch nothing until we hear her story." Then, he turned to Calli his voice still ringing with authority, "You stay here and help Lilly. We'll meet you both back at Matt's later." Jax stares at them until they nod their assent and leave to find Matt.

THE HOMANI MALE, hearing their plan, slips back into the shadows unnoticed. He is unobtrusively making his way to the collapsed bar top. Spying what he needs, he reaches down and pockets the one thing that could connect him to the events of the evening. A moment of regret floods him for Dawn, but he quickly shakes it off as a necessary means to an end for his master plan. *Fools! Blind fools!* He raged in his thoughts. *I'll force them to see the bitch for who she is! The apple doesn't fall far from the tree. I'll show them. I'll show all of them what blood runs through her veins. Evil! Tainted! They shall see! They shall see!* His maniacal rant, a running loop in his head, as he sneaks out the back emergency exit into the night.

SHIFTING INTO HIS TIGER, Jax follows the tracks left by Matt and Dawn into the nearby woods. He is panting heavily from a hard run when he stumbles upon them a few miles in. Matt is sitting on the ground, leaning his back against a large pine while a still agitated Dawn paces naked in human form.

Cuts and bruises rapidly heal on both of them, evidence of the fight Dawn has given Matt.

Sidling up to Matt, Jax lets his tiger go and walks the rest of the way in human form. Matt puts his fingers to his lips in a shushing motion as he studies Dawn's behavior.

"Has she said anything yet?" Jax whispers to Matt, not wanting to disturb Dawn.

Eyes not leaving her, Matt whispers, "No, she just let her wolf go. She's been pacing and mumbling about flowers in the cage. She's physically back, but mentally," he shrugs, "mentally, whatever caused this, still has her. So I'm letting her work it out of her system."

Jax slides down to sit by Matt, waiting for their friend to return to them.

THE FRONT DOOR opening startles Calli from her deep slumber on the couch. The morning sun has lit the room with its glow. Her gaze briefly meets Lilly, who has been watching over her while she sleeps.

Both women jump up and rush to the two haggard, naked men who escort a blanket-covered Dawn into the room.

No longer bothered by the sight of public nudity, Calli reaches for Matt, who envelopes her in an exhausted hug.

"Is she going to be okay?" she whispers in his ear. Matt gives a quick nod as reply as Lilly hands him and Jax blankets from the nearby couch.

After taking a seat, silence reigns for a few minutes, heavy in the air, before Matt speaks. "From what Dawn has told us," he starts, glancing at Dawn, who nods permission to tell her story, "her night started out as usual. The bar got slammed. The next thing she remembered was being overcome by an uncontrollable rage. After that, everything was blank until about thirty minutes ago."

Jax, Matt, and Lilly share a look of understanding. Lilly lets out a slight keening sound and shrinks in on herself.

Calli, noticing her friend's distress, is confused. She looks at him. "What aren't you saying, Matt?"

"When Dawn first shifted back, she kept mumbling

about flowers in the cage. I didn't figure it out until just before she came around. When we were in the facility, the scientists sometimes used Monkshood flowers to bring forth our animals and make us fight," he finishes, leaning forward with his elbows on his knees, rubbing his hands through his hair.

Calli recoils in horror. "How could they do that to you? You were just children!".

Jax lets out a tired sigh. "They didn't care, Calli. We were just property to them. A means to an end."

Clearing her throat, Lilly joins the conversation. "It was cruel. We didn't realize what we were doing until afterwards. We became pure animals. They would pit friends against friends, sometimes family members. It was usually a fight to the death," she ends in a whisper.

With tears streaming down her face, Calli looks over at Dawn. "I'm so sorry. Are you okay?"

Dawn glances up. Her usually mischievous grin is absent. In its place, her mouth is a tension-filled tight line. "I will be when I find out who did this to me. Then I want first rights, Matt," she demands with venom.

Matt notices Calli's confusion. "It's part of our laws. If a Homani harms another Homani, they have the first right to decide their punishment." Then, looking back at Dawn, he solemnly swears, "First rights you shall have."

Rising from her seat, Dawn nods her thanks as she heads towards the door. Jax jumps up to trail after her. "I'll stay with her tonight."

Lilly rises from her chair. "I'll be leaving now that you're home." Pausing at the door, she turns to Matt. "Find the fucker who did this. Death is too good for them."

Matt wraps Calli in his arms once they're alone. Calli

exhales wearily, "Matt, who would do something like this? It doesn't make sense."

"I don't know, but I will find out," he promises as he kisses her temple and steers them towards their bedroom upstairs. They are so exhausted by the events of the night, sleep quickly claims them both.

FOURTEEN

The feel of Matt's muscled arm wrapped around her as she spoons into him is Calli's favorite way to wake up. Squirming her ass against him, the feel of his steel rod pushing up against her has her juices flowing.

Matt's light snores rumble faintly in the room. Slowly turning to face him, Calli works her way down his body, taking her time to enjoy the ridges of his muscles. Upon admiring his naked body, Calli wraps her hand around his shaft, bringing it to her lips. Flattening her tongue, she licks him from base to tip, dipping her tongue in his slit at the top before taking his head into her mouth.

Matt's groan and the sudden feel of his hand in her hair encourage her to continue. Then, using her tongue to lubricate his smooth shaft, Calli relaxes her throat and takes him deep, her mouth stretching wide to accommodate him.

Breathing through her nose, the scent of sandalwood fills her senses. Reaching down with her other hand, Calli works a finger into her drenched channel as she uses her thumb on her clit. Matt's hand tightens in her hair as she increases her pace on his silken rod, hollowing her cheeks as she sucks him hard, swirling her tongue around the tip before taking him deeply once again.

"Fuck Calli, I love your mouth. Take it all. I want you to swallow me down," he pants.

His words spur her on. Calli increases her pace, tightening her hand on his rock-hard shaft as she struggles to take him deeper. The throbbing between her legs increases with her speed as she finger fucks herself to the edge.

Pulling back with a pop, Calli's eyes meet Matt's. "I need you to cum. I'm almost there," she pleads, taking him deep in her throat.

Thrusting his hips as he pushes the back of her head down on him more, his member swells to an almost unmanageable size. Sucking his pre-cum, Calli's clit pulses rapidly and her body tenses as she explodes around her hand. The sound of her cumming triggers Matt's release, shooting deep into her throat.

Pulling her up to him, he kisses her thoroughly, then grabs her hand to lick off her juices from her fingers. "Hmmm, I love the taste of you." he hums as he pops the last finger out of his mouth.

Their lips meet again, and Calli enjoys the feel of his morning stubble on her cheeks. Not to be outdone, Matt rolls her over and begins sucking on her perky pink nipple, plucking the other with his hand. "I think this one's my favorite," he says between nibbles.

"You can't have a favorite, Matt. The other one would get jealous," she giggles at their play.

"Well, we can't have that!" he says as he buries his face between her ample breasts, biting one nipple, then the other.

Their laughter dies down as their desire rises. Matt raises

himself above Calli and stares at her with a heated gaze, his eyes shining more turquoise than teal.

"I'm going to take you hard and fast. I need to be inside that sweet tight pussy," Matt warns Calli as he lines himself up with her opening and slides himself to the hilt. His balls slap against her ass.

As turned on as Calli is, her sopping pussy is ready for his deep thrust. His width causes a slight burn as it stretches her to her limit. Arching her head back as she exposes her throat to Matt, her body is on fire from being so full.

"Fuck Calli, my animal is too close to the surface. Don't fucking move!" He exclaims. Taking advantage of her submissive pose, Matt leans forward as he bites between her neck and shoulder, holding her in place. His wolf demands complete submission from his mate.

Calli stills her movements. Her nipples harden at the excitement of bringing Matt so close to losing control. A flush spreads over her body as a rush of desire consumes her.

Matt's deep strokes became erratic, his hips bucking hard as he drove his shaft into her repeatedly. The angle of his thrust caused his cock to rub against her g-spot, the swelling nerves alight and ready to burst.

Sweat covers them in a fine film as their mutual peak comes rushing towards them. Matt thrusts one last time with a deep growl, his member pulsing as he coats her insides with his cum. The throbbing of his release triggers Calli's own as she squeezes her eyes closed, fireworks exploding behind her lids.

After licking the bite mark on her neck, Matt rests his forehead on hers, his heavy breathing matching hers. Staring into her eyes, his love clear, Matt quickly kisses her swollen lips. "You're going to be the death of me, but I'd die a lucky man."

Laying her head on his chest, Calli enjoys the sound of the steady rhythm of his heartbeat. Her thoughts drift to the night before. "What are you going to do, Matt?"

Tension at her inquiry causes his muscles to tighten under her. "Jax and I will question Dawn again, see if she remembers anything else. He's going to the bar today to find any potential clues. That's all we can do."

Squeezing her, he kisses her forehead. "You, my love, are coming with me today."

"I have an afternoon shift at the diner today. Maverick's off at three," she reminds him.

Kissing the top of her head, "I'll have you back in time. I'm taking you to the Dam."

She jumps up with a squeal, "Really? I'm so excited to finally meet Harold and Peter!"

"Well, you would have met them sooner if you hadn't painted Jax," Matt laughs as she throws a pillow at him.

"Go get ready, trouble," he says, swatting her ass playfully.

FIFTEEN

The long winding roads to the dam give Calli an appreciation for the large territory of the Homani. She has seen the enormous fields that yield their crops but hasn't ventured away from the town after her encounter in the woods.

Seeing the enormous expanse of forest, her breath hitches when it opens onto a beautiful lake. The waters are calm, almost glass-like in appearance, as the colourful fall trees reflect off the surface.

Finally, the dam itself comes into view. A wall of concrete slices through the lake, joining the opposite side of the forest at the narrowest point.

Driving the truck across the top of the dam, Matt stops halfway and parks near a shack-like structure. Two older men emerge from the door to the shack. *This must be Harold and Pete,* Calli muses. Their weathered skin belies their age as the two spry men jostle each other like children to reach the truck first. They remove their ball caps out of respect as they approach before greeting Calli.

Thrusting a gnarled hand forward, Pete is the first to introduce himself.

"Ma'am, it's a pleasure to meet the woman who stole Matt's heart," he says. His brown eyes glow with pride when he looks at Matt.

Harold, not to be outdone, elbows him out of the way and bows slightly at Calli. He takes her hand and raises it to his lips, pausing when a low growl comes from Matt.

"Hush, boy! You know I don't mean no harm to your mate. Manners and a little southern charm go a long way," Harold chastises Matt.

Laughing at their antics, Calli instantly falls in love with the two men who helped save and raise the Homani. "It is an honor to meet you both."

Clapping Matt on the back, Pete gives him a wink. "You done did good, boy, you done did good!" Mollified by their immediate acceptance of Calli, Matt leads the way down the stairs to the heart of the dam.

The continuous sound of water dripping has Calli on edge as they make their way through the dimly lit passageways. "Uh, is that normal?" She asks, pointing to a spot where water is steadily pouring through a crack onto the floor.

Harold slaps the concrete wall hard with his hand. "She's strong as an ox. She may be a bit long in the tooth, but she's solid," he says with pride, speaking of the dam like an old friend.

Feeling reassured, Calli continues following the men into what looks like a vast maintenance room. The smell of grease and metal surrounds her in the stale air.

Turning on a hanging light, Harold, Peter, and Matt stand discussing the large metal box on the table. Not understanding the jargon they are using, Calli wanders around the room, amazed at the unique equipment that keeps the dam running and the lights on in the town.

Calli remembers stories her mom had told her of cities that were lit so bright that they could be seen from space and ways for people to communicate worldwide instantly.

This was how the world learned of the secret facilities and experiments. The public's outrage had been palpable, and the riots had begun. Small at first, then country against country. Finally, someone pressed the button, and nuclear war and its fallout eradicated eighty percent of the population. Most of our technology was destroyed, and so many lives were lost.

A great sadness fills her as she wanders from one machine to the next.

Noticing her curiosity, Pete approaches Calli and begins explaining what each machine did and how they were all connected. Grateful for the impromptu tutorial, Calli absorbs as much information as possible. After a while, Matt's walkie-talkie crackles to life.

"Matt, April here. Is Calli going to make her shift? Maverick is acting antsy. It's making the customers nervous."

"On our way now, April. We lost track of time out here at the Dam. You might want to be careful, or Harold and Pete may try to steal Calli away from you. She picked up on the runnings of this place pretty quick," he chuckles as April starts swearing a blue streak over the line.

"And furthermore, you tell those two old coots they'll never get an extra slice of pie from me if they try that bull-shit!" April winds down.

Grabbing the receiver from Matt, who is bent over laughing at the look of horror on Pete and Harold's faces, Calli quickly reassures April that she is on her way.

Calli slaps Matt's rock-hard chest. "Ouch! Shit, Matt.

April's the sweetest person I know, but I have seen her temper. Don't fuck with her like that!"

With a quick goodbye to the elderly gentlemen, Matt and Calli speed down the road to the diner.

Tires screeching to a halt, Calli quickly kisses Matt as she jumps out of the truck's cab and rushes into the diner. Grabbing her apron off its hook and tying it around her waist, Calli barrels into the kitchen, coming to an abrupt halt as she bounces off Maverick's back.

With inhuman speed, Maverick spins and grabs Calli's upper arms, his grip biting painfully. Calli tries to pull away with a pained moan, only to be forcefully pulled towards him. Maverick's eyes shine a bright turquoise.

He pulls her close, his breath a whisper on her face. "Be careful, Calli. We wouldn't want you to get hurt," he growls before he shoves her away. Stumbling in shock at his ominous words and rough handling of her, Calli stands still, speechless. Maverick shakes his head, his eyes now teal once again.

He takes a step towards Calli, his face scrunched in remorse. "I'm so sorry. Forgive me. I - I need to go see Lilly."

He rushes past her out of the kitchen, leaving her gaping after him. Calli stands frozen until the sudden arrival of April shakes her out of her stupor.

"Oh, thank god you're here! The dinner rush is starting." April's words spur Calli into motion. She shakes off the unsettling encounter and busies herself with preparing the meal for the hungry diners.

CHAPTER

SIXTEEN

Working side by side with April as they clear down the kitchen post diner rush, a loud crash from the dining room startles both women. Rushing to investigate, they stop abruptly inside the room as a plate flies by their heads, crashing into the back wall. The diners, some in human form, others in their animal form, are squared off, earth-shaking growls and shouts filling the room.

April quickly unclips the handset on her belt with shaky hands as she sends out a distress call. "Matt! Jax! Get to the diner quickly! They've all gone feral! Help!"

Matt's angry response is immediate, "Lock yourselves in the walk-in. We're on our way!"

Grabbing Calli by the arm as the first attack begins, April rushes them to the walk-in refrigerator and hits the emergency lock. The women can hear the destruction through the thick walls as the Homani rip into each other in a violent frenzy.

Wide-eyed, Calli clings to April, both trembling with fear while they wait. Soon, they hear the muffled staccato pops of a tranquilizer gun, letting them know that the cavalry had arrived.

The ensuing silence is deafening. Then, a knock on the outside of the door startles them both. Matt's calm voice soon follows. "You can come out now."

Opening the door, Calli rushes to Matt. The comforting feel of his arms wrapping around her staunch the flow of tears that streak down her face.

"Is everyone okay?" Calli's voice, hoarse from crying, asks into Matt's chest.

He gives her a reassuring squeeze, "For now. We had to tranquilize them. Jax and Lilly are bringing the injured to the clinic. They will restrain the rest until we figure it out."

Glaring at April, Matt's tone takes on an authoritative timber. "What the fuck happened?"

Ducking her head in submission, April's voice quivers as she speaks. "I don't know. Calli and I were wiping down the kitchen after the dinner run when all hell broke loose."

At that moment, Jax pops his head into the kitchen. "Matt, you need to hear this." He gestures to the dining area.

Entering the room, a lone Homani sits with a dazed look on her face. The gash above her brow is crusted with blood from her rapid healing. Looking up as they approach, the middle-aged woman shrinks back in fear.

"Shhh, it's alright, Thelma," Lilly soothes her. "Tell Matt what you told Jax and me, okay?"

Thelma raises her fear-filled eyes to Matt. "It was the cages all over again, Matt. I could feel the sudden rush of anger and then the loss of control."

Snapping his head in April's direction, he barks out, "What was served tonight? Did everyone have the same order?"

Nervously rubbing the hem of her apron, April quickly glances at Calli. "Uh, yeah. It was the 'Calli Special,' her chicken pot pie. It's a big hit, so yeah, everyone ordered it."

Stiffening at her words, Matt orders Lilly to get a sample and bring it to the doctor safely. "Maybe Doc can configure what's in it. Then, hopefully, he can create an antidote."

Running his hands through his hair in frustration, Matt turns to Calli. "I need to go to the clinic and speak with Doc. I'll drop you off at the house and post a guard outside until I get back."

"You don't think I had anything to do with this, do you?" Hurt is apparent in her voice.

"No, babe. It's for your safety. Unfortunately, there have been some rumblings among some townspeople, and I'm not taking any chances," he sighs, hugging her.

It devastates Calli to hear that people suspect her of such treachery. Slumping in defeat, she nods as Matt leads her to the truck.

MATT PULLS into the parking lot of the clinic. A gathering of townspeople is waiting, milling about the front of the building. Putting the gearshift into park, He sits for a minute, rubbing his temples as the beginning of a tension headache takes hold. With a deep sigh, he exits his truck and walks toward the entrance.

"Matt! MATT!" a bystander shouts. "What are you doing to stop this? Are we safe?"

The fear rolls off of the crowd, blasting him in waves. He

raises his hands to quiet them down. "Look, I understand your concerns. We're doing everything we can to sort this out. But I need you all to go home and stay there until we sort this out."

Reluctantly heeding his order, the crowd disperses. Making his way into the clinic, Matt goes in search of Doc. They have lined beds along the walls, two deep, as people lay either still tranquilized or fastened in restraints for their protection and the protection of others. He can still hear snarls and low growls coming from some as they fight through the effects of the poison.

A harried-looking elderly gentleman with glasses perching precariously on the top of his head rounds the corner.

"Doc!" Matt yells to get his attention. "Any news on the sample Lilly brought you?"

"For the love that's all holy, Matt. Lilly just gave it to me a half hour ago. I'm not a damn miracle worker!" he responds in frustration.

"I know, I know. Sorry," he says, looking around at the chaos. "I need answers."

"And I need you to get out of my way," Doc responds, brushing past Matt to quickly readjust the restraints on a patient. "When I have something, I'll let you know. Right now, making sure these people survive and not kill each other is my priority."

"If they say anything when they come around, let me know immediately, please," Matt requests politely, knowing that with Doc, he'd catch more flies with honey than vinegar. He heads towards the exit to find Jax waiting for him at the truck. His usual quick smile and good looks, are creased with strain.

Shifting from one foot to the next, Jax avoids Matt's eyes

as he approaches. "We have some news. Dawn remembered something."

Matt could hear the apprehension in Jax's tone, stilling at his words. "What is it?" he demands, his wolf riding him to lash out.

"Just follow me back to your place. Lilly and Dawn are waiting," he says as he hops back into the cab of his truck.

The guard Matt has stationed at the house is sitting on the front porch. His animal is close to the surface, and his turquoise eyes narrow at Matt's approach.

Grabbing Matt by the arm, Jax tries to rush him into the house, but not before the guard mutters, "This is your fault."

With lightning speed, Matt swings around and grabs the guard by his throat. Lifting him off the ground, Matt leans in and whispers. "What do you mean, my fault?" His voice held a promise of death.

"Matt! Let him go. We have bigger problems. Come on," Jax yells from the entryway.

With a final warning shake, Matt drops the guard. Walking over him as he lay gasping for breath.

The living room is tension-filled when Matt enters. Lilly and Dawn are sitting across from each other. Lilly's glare has Dawn lowering her eyes.

Glancing around, Matt takes in the scene, a pit forming in his stomach. "Where's Calli?" he barks.

"She's upstairs for now. Take a seat, Matt. You need to hear this." Jax sits on the couch, taking Dawn's hand in his own.

Raising a brow at Jax's actions, Matt moves to the over-stuffed chair facing them. He leans forward with his elbows on his knees, steepling his fingers. "Okay, Dawn. What do you remember?"

With a reassuring nod from Jax, Dawn begins, "Cookies."

"Cookies?" Matt's eyes drill into hers.

"Yes, cookies. The night at the bar, I could smell cookies when Calli ordered their drinks. She said they were a treat for you, but I begged her for them. Not long after I ate them, I lost control," Dawn finishes in a whisper, not wanting to meet Matt's eyes.

Her implication hangs like a heavy fog in the room. Matt's heart constricts painfully, a vice in his chest.

Bursting from her chair, Lilly is shaking with anger, her eyes glowing. "There's no fucking way Calli has anything to do with this! I refuse to believe it."

Jax ran his hand through his long, golden hair. "Lil," he starts, "I don't want to believe it, but these poisonings happened after she arrived."

"Coincidence!" Lilly interrupts. "Or someone is trying to pin it on her."

"C'mon, Lilly. You have to admit; she's had ample opportunity. We don't know anything about her. The cookies were meant for Matt, for fuck's sake!" Jax ends his argument with a roar.

"Oh really, Jax? When the fuck has she ever been alone? If you're not with her," Lilly points a finger at Jax, "then either Matt, April, or I am!" She crosses her arms and stares him down.

"ENOUGH!" Matt bellows, his eyes narrowing. "Be careful, Jax, that's my mate you're accusing!"

"Your *human* mate, Matt. I know you love her. Hell, everyone loves Calli, but can she be trusted? If it were anyone else, you'd haul them to the barn for interrogation!" Jax looks to the heavens in frustration. "I'm just giving voice to what other people are whispering, Matt. Don't shoot the fucking messenger."

A cry from the stairs has them turn towards Calli, who stands frozen. Her hand covers her quivering lips as silent tears stream down her face. Her wide eyes search out Matt.

"You don't believe this, do you?" she implores him.

Standing to take a step towards her, then pausing, Matt sighs heavily, "I don't want to doubt your loyalty, Calli, but Jax is right. If it were anyone else, I would question them. But I can't let my feelings for you blind me."

"No! No fucking way, Matt!" Lilly leaps in front of Calli. "You're blinded, alright, but not by Calli. This smells of a set-up, and I'm going to fucking prove it!"

Grabbing Calli's hand, Lilly places herself between the two men, keeping Calli close to her back as they make their way out of the house.

The guard outside tries to block Lilly, who spins around, her leg flying out, catching his chin, and knocking him out cold.

After putting a distraught Calli in her truck, Lilly rounds on Matt, who stands on the porch. "Find the truth, Matt. Until then, Calli will be safe with me. When you get your head out of your ass and want to beg her forgiveness, you know where she'll be. Not that you deserve her." Lilly spits out, then revs the engine and speeds down the street.

SEVENTEEN

Wandering through his empty house, Matt's heart is breaking. He misses Calli. Her off-key humming as she cooks, how her face would light up when he came home, and holding her in his arms at night.

Seven long nights since he has been away from her. It feels like an eternity. Entering the bedroom she used when she first arrived, Matt inhales deeply. Calli's vanilla and lavender scent are still faint in the air.

Sitting on the end of the bed, Matt calls himself all kinds of a fool for ever doubting his mate. Ultimately, he knows his distrust is not in Calli, but in his own ability to remain impartial when it comes to her. Jax was right in the sense that he needs a clear head in order to figure out who has been putting the community at risk. *Jax is fucking wrong though, without my mate by my side, I can't think clearly.* Standing up abruptly, ready to charge to Lilly's to win her back, Matt hears a crinkle underfoot.

Looking down, Matt notices a yellowed piece of paper

peeking half out from under the bed. Picking it up, his muscled legs give way, and he sits down hard on the bed as he reads the faded headline of the newspaper article.

His eyes widen as he stares at an image of Calli. No, not Calli, her mother? The resemblance is uncanny. Rising quickly, his heart beating frantically in his chest, Matt runs for the door with the newspaper clipping crumpled tightly in his fist.

THE BANGING on the door startles Calli, causing the drink she is holding to slosh over her hand. Taking her drink and handing Calli a napkin, Lilly winks at her. "I told you, hun, that man would come around quickly. Don't forgive him too fast. Make him sweat a bit for his assholery."

Calli sits up, using the napkin to dry the tears that have run down her cheeks. A moment later, the door bursts open. Matt stands there, his dark hair a wild mess, muscles bulging from his wolf so close to the surface.

In a barely human voice, he growls at Lilly. "Get Jax over here now!" Then, turning his glowing turquoise eyes on Calli, he points. "You have some fucking explaining to do!" The intensity of his anger has Calli recoiling, her fear palpable.

A hand on Matt's arm has him whipping in Lilly's direction. "DON'T! For once, do as I fucking say!"

Slowly stepping back from Matt, her head down in a submissive pose, Lilly reaches for her walkie-talkie to call for Jax. Glancing at Calli, she whispers, "Calli, I've never seen Matt in this out of control. Don't make any sudden movements. We must wait for Jax in case Matt loses complete control of his wolf." Both women watch as Matt paces back and forth in the foyer.

An eternity later, Jax's truck came to a screeching halt in front of Lilly's. Rushing through the open doorway, Jax stops dead in his tracks at the sight of Matt pacing, more wolf than human noises escaping him.

"Was he poisoned?" Jax whispers to Lilly, keeping a cautious eye on Matt.

As if coming out of a trance, Matt turns to Jax. "No, I wasn't poisoned. I was fucking betrayed - by her!" Matt roars, pointing at Calli, then tosses the balled-up newspaper at Lilly's feet.

With a shaky hand, Lilly reaches down and picks up the crumpled yellow paper, smoothing it out on the table next to her. Quickly scanning the article, Lilly lets out a gasp. Then, looking up at Calli, her eyes filled with hurt and confusion.

"What is this? Calli, explain what this is, please?" she begs.

A knife-like pain stabs through Calli's chest as sweat breaks out over her tingling body. Her breathing is rapid as an anxiety attack tries to take hold.

"Oh, no, no, no, no, no."

Jax pulls the paper out of Lilly's hand, his handsome face paling as he reads. Then, with accusing eyes, he growls at Calli, "Who the fuck are you?"

Calli clasps her hands and closes her eyes, taking slow, deep breaths to calm herself. Once in control, she looks up at the three sets of eyes staring daggers.

"It's not what you think," she starts slowly, "my mother was married to Dr. Brent Jameson. I refuse to acknowledge him as anything other than the sperm donor that impregnated my mom."

Calli glances at Matt, her eyes pleading. "My mother stumbled upon his scientific reports and videos. The torture, killing and forced birth, not to mention the cruel testing of the Homani who survived the accelerated growth, among other horrors." Calli pauses to catch her breath through her choking cry.

"She took the information public. The government tried to cover it up, but she had the evidence to back it up and distributed it wide before she went into hiding. What that article doesn't say is how we were hunted by various governments and investors whom she destroyed by outing them."

All three sink onto the couch in stunned silence at her last words. Each of them digesting what Calli has said. Both men seem to have deflated, and Lilly is watching her with shining eyes.

Lilly is the first to speak. "You were as much a victim as we were."

Calli bursts up from her chair, "NO! Don't you see? My mother was the catalyst for the Great Release, the destruction of our world! That bastard she married killed and tortured so many people! All of you!" Calli points at them. Sucking in a shuddering breath she bangs on her chest, "It's my family's fault!"

"But Calli, you were just a child. What they did isn't on you." Matt says in a low voice as he rises to comfort her.

Backing away, Calli holds her hands up, tears streaming down her face.

"Momma always said we were to blame. That we didn't deserve to survive. That bad blood ran through my veins from that monster," she chokes out.

Lightening fast, Matt snatches Calli into his arms, clinging her struggling body to his. "Oh baby girl, your mother was wrong. She put her guilt on you, which wasn't right."

Sobbing into Matt's chest, Calli feels Lilly and Jax's hands rubbing her back in comfort.

"I'm sorry for ever doubting you, Calli," Jax speaks first, his voice thick with emotion.

"We're your family now," Lilly murmurs. "You're a good person with a loving heart. There's no evil in you. So don't let her words colour who you truly are."

Choking back tears, Calli meets their gaze. "How could you forgive me? I don't deserve it."

Matt squeezes her tight, kissing the top of her head. "There's nothing to forgive. We love you. I love you. I was a fool ever to doubt my mate. Can you forgive me?" he asks, his voice hoarse with unshed tears.

Reaching up, Calli brings Matt's mouth to hers. "I love you so fucking much it hurts," he says before their lips meet.

Their kiss is long and sensual. It is a homecoming of two hearts reuniting, sealing the cracks in a bond almost broken by secrets and misunderstanding. Coming up for air, Matt steers Calli towards the door.

"We'll keep Calli's past between us for now," he warns Jax and Lilly. "Until we understand who's behind the poisonings, we don't want anyone to jump to conclusions."

The three share a look, knowing not everyone will be so forgiving of her past. Jax and Lilly nod in agreement as Matt and Calli leave.

THE SHADOWY FIGURE ducks back down into the bushes under the window. The conversation he has been eavesdropping on infuriates him. His muscles bulge as waves of rage roll through him.

NO! FOOLS! That bitch will pay for the sins of her father! BLIND! They're all blind to her treachery! Forgiveness, he spits on the ground, *is for the weak. If they don't do what must be done, I will!* His animal overtakes him, and he runs into the nearby forest, planning his next move.

THEY MAKE the drive to the house in silence. Matt holds Calli's small, soft hand in his callous one. When they pull up to the house, he kisses her knuckles as a sign of encouragement. "Come on. It's been a long night."

Walking into the house, a sense of homecoming fills Calli with Matt by her side. Her past is no longer a heavy burden upon her shoulders.

Leading him upstairs, Calli pauses in their room. Her emerald eyes shine with unshed tears. "Thank you for believing in me."

Matt pulls Calli to stand between his legs as he sits on the bed. He lifts her chin, looking directly in her eyes. His voice is thick with emotion as he tells her, "Don't thank me Calli. I don't deserve it. I never should have doubted you to begin with. This I will promise, I will be a better mate. One you deserve."

Matt envelopes Calli in a hug, his muscles shivering with tension. With a tender kiss, he seals his promise.

EIGHTEEN

Sitting at the table having breakfast, Matt's walkie-talkie crackles to life.

"Matt, Doc here. I think I found something. Can you come to the clinic?"

"On our way," he replies, meeting Calli's eyes.

The drive through town is eerily quiet. The streets are bare of residents, afraid to leave their homes. Most of the shops have closed for the day, apprehensive about being the next target.

Calli grips Matt's hand. "It's like a ghost town," she whispers nervously.

"The townspeople are scared, rightfully so. But, we'll get to the bottom of this." Matt kisses her knuckles, his lips a comforting warmth on her hand.

The clinic is blessedly empty of patients. The Homani who had been poisoned had all recovered physically. However, the psychological effects of being reminded of the cages would take a while to overcome.

At the front desk sits a heavily scarred Homani. One of

the guards, Calli surmises by his uniform. Looking up from the desk, he greets Matt with a nod. "Hey, Matt."

"Hey, Ben."

When Ben's gaze turns to Calli, his eyes narrow, filled with suspicion.

"Do we have a problem here?" Matt demands, his eyes glowing.

Ben spits on the floor, "No. Just keep your pet human on a leash."

Without warning, Matt grabs Ben by the throat, hauling him over the desk and slams him to the floor. Then, with his heavy boot on Ben's throat, Matt leans down and growls, "You want to repeat that?" He adds a little more pressure, causing Ben's face to turn a bluish hue.

"I - I didn't mean anything. Please, Matt," Ben gasps from the floor. With a swift kick to the face, Matt knocks Ben out cold.

"I see I have a new patient," Doc remarks drolly as he leans against the wall, watching Matt exact punishment to his guard.

Matt walks over to where Calli is standing. Her hand covers her mouth with a horrified look on her face. "C'mon babe, don't waste your pity on Ben. He got what he deserved. A lesson learned and a reminder of who leads this town."

Doc nods his agreement. "Calli, the animal side of the Homani, needs structure. A hierarchy, if you will. Matt, being the elected leader of this community, must maintain his dominance and mete out punishment swiftly or, quite frankly, chaos would ensue from having a weak leader."

Calli walks into Matt's waiting arms. His strength surrounds her. "What did you find out, Doc?" Matt asks as they walk towards the clinic's lab, leaving the unconscious Ben on the floor for maintenance to deal with.

As they walk through the lab door, Doc hurries over to a vial placed carefully in a glass cabinet.

"I was able to extract the poison from the sample Lilly brought me," he begins with excitement. "You were right in your initial assessment. It's monkshood."

"I don't understand. Monkshood is native here. It grows wild in the meadows, isn't that what you said?" she asks Matt.

"It does," Doc answers for Matt. "We can walk among it. But, we need to be careful not to rub against it. The oil absorption from the flower on our skin causes the feral reaction you witnessed. Too much would cause cardiac arrest and death."

Turning to Calli, Matt explains, "When we were in the facility, scientists put monkshood flowers in our cages. Increasing the amount to study the effects. There was no room to move without it touching us."

"If ingested in a micro-dose," Doc continues, "the feral behavior would be a likely response."

"How difficult is it to extract the oil from the flower?" Calli inquires.

"Not difficult at all. It's the same cold press procedure we use for essential oils," Doc shrugs.

"Is there anything we can do for the people who have already been affected?" Matt asks with concern.

His face lit up. "Yes, actually! I was able to use activated charcoal on the infected Homani. It prevented the absorption of most of the monkshood in their gastrointestinal tract, and our nanobots enhanced the elimination of the rest."

Matt claps Doc on the back. His enthusiasm sends the elderly Homani forward a few steps. Calli reaches out to steady him. "Geez, Matt! Careful with the enthusiasm!" she chuckles as Doc rights himself.

With a look of censure at Matt, Doc walks over to another cabinet that houses hundreds of black vials. "I made enough antidote for the town. I would suggest having Dawn go door to door to deliver it. She's been a victim of this and a trusted community member. People will be more apt to take something with her assurance."

Matt grunts his approval as he and Calli leave the clinic.

NINETEEN

As the days pass, the town returns to its usual bustling nature. The Homani, now armed with an antidote, no longer fear leaving their homes and living their lives. Children happily fill the playground with laughter now that the school has reopened. The businesses swing their doors wide, welcoming shoppers into their buildings, delighted to return to normal.

Jax, Lilly, Matt, Calli, and Dawn meet at Dawn's bar. The only business yet to open, as the bar is still under construction, repairing the damage that was done. Being closed to the public gives the group the privacy they need.

"It pisses me off that we still have no leads." Jax sinks back in his chair as he runs his long fingers through his hair, then takes a drink of his beer.

Dawn throws back her shot of tequila, "You're not the only one." she commiserates with Jax.

"We need a way to draw this asshole out in the open. Get them to tip their hand," Calli says.

"How?" Matt replies.

Leaning forward, Lilly looks each of them in the eye. "I have an idea, but you're not going to like it," she finishes, staring directly at Matt.

Matt stiffens in his seat, "Oh fuck no!"

Calli grabs Matt's arm. "What's going on?"

"Lilly wants to use you as bait," he states flatly.

"Me? Why me?" Calli asks, confused.

Lilly heaves a sigh as she reaches out to clasp Calli's hand in hers. "I have had my suspicions that this was about you from the start. The timing of the poisoning shortly after your arrival, the fuelling of the gossip to the townspeople. Whoever is doing this has something against you, personally. I have a few suspects in mind, but without proof, I have nothing."

Matt leaps to his feet. "Just fucking tell me who you think it is, Lilly, and I'll beat it out of them and leave the rest for my wolf!" His eyes flared turquoise.

Calli sits quietly as she traces her finger along the grooves of the wooden table. Jax, Dawn, Lilly and Matt argue around her. Their voices are raised, each trying to sway the other.

"I'll do it," Calli whispers. Their Homani hearing catches her words as if she has shouted them.

"The hell you will!" Matt bellows.

A calmness has descended upon Calli as she looks up at the man she loves. "Don't you see? Lilly's right. It has to be me. I need to do this for the safety of all the Homani." Her eyes widen as she pleads with him.

Matt wraps his arms around Calli from behind her chair. Leaning down, he whispers in her ear. "I understand that you still have some misplaced guilt, babe. But you have done nothing wrong. So you don't need absolution."

Grateful that he understands her, Calli tilts her head and

kisses Matt. "You all may believe that, but someone out there doesn't, and they need to be stopped," she says, her voice firm.

When no one argues, Calli leans forward, her elbows on the table. "What's the plan?"

CHAPTER

TWENTY

The truck rolls to a stop in front of the diner. Matt glances at the large front window, giving him a perfect view of the packed restaurant. Turning to Calli, he notices her slight trembling. "We don't have to do this. We can find another way," he says.

"No. Let's just get this part over with," Calli sighs as she pulls the handle on the truck door and walks towards the diner.

The smell of freshly baked goods and coffee calm Calli as she moves behind the counter. She grabs her apron and ties it around her waist as she prepares for her shift.

April approaches her. "Glad to see you're back," she gestures to the full booths. "We have a full house for dinner service tonight. I think everyone is relieved to leave their homes for a change."

Matt sits at the counter, idly playing with the menu in his hands.

"What can I get you?" April asks him, her smile bright.

"I'll have the 'Calli Special.'" His voice is slightly raised for all to hear.

Calli's gasp echoes through the now-silent diner as all eyes turn in her direction. A mixture of emotions, surprise, suspicion and anger is displayed on the faces of the diners.

"Matt, you know we took that off the menu," April says with caution as she glances at the onlookers with trepidation.

Matt raps his knuckles on the countertop. "If Calli's my mate, then she needs to toughen up." Looking over his shoulder at the crowd he adds, "she needs to stand up for herself."

A coffee cup whizzes by Matt's head as he ducks.

Anger flashes in Calli's eyes as she picks up another cup. "IF? *If* I'm your mate?" she yells as she throws the second cup.

"Toughen up?" she bellows, her face red as the third cup narrowly misses Matt.

"Fuck you! You arrogant prick!" Calli screams as she removes her apron and heads for the door.

"I hope Jax has a couch you can sleep on, don't you fucking think of coming home tonight!" Calli rounds on Matt before she storms out the door.

April narrows her eyes at Matt. "What the fuck is wrong with you?" She glares as she follows Calli outside.

"Hey, Calli! Wait up! I'll drive you home." April hollers to Calli, who is stomping down the street.

Calli hops into the truck and turns to April. "Think they bought it?"

April giggles. "Oh girl, I thought for sure Matt would need stitches. Good thing your aim was off."

Calli raises an eyebrow. "Oh, darlin' if I had wanted to hit him, that coffee cup would have hit its mark," she laughs.

April shuts the truck off in front of the house. "Everyone in place?"

"Yeah, Jax shifted into his tiger. With his superior hearing, he'll know if anyone comes around. Lilly's panther is prowling the back, also on alert," Calli says with a nervous edge to her voice.

"Okay, good. I'll return to the diner and keep Matt there until he's needed," April says in exasperation, knowing that would be the most challenging part of this plan.

"Go on in, take a bath, pour a glass of wine-the usual post-fight routine. If you're being watched, it will be predictable behavior."

With a nod, Calli left the truck and walked into the house. In the bathroom, she runs a tub, then goes to the kitchen and pours herself a glass of wine. She keeps her movements steady even though she is shaking inside.

Hidden well, as he was trained to do, the man pulls back into the shadows. An evil smile appears on his otherwise handsome face. *Poor little girl, have your friends abandoned you? Has your mate come to his senses? Soon I'll have you, and you will pay! Come out, come out, Calli! It's time to play!*

As she makes her way upstairs, Calli's startled as the front door bursts open. Calli scrambles up the stairs with a scream, a hand latching onto her ankle, hauling her down hard on the wood. Swinging around, Calli's eyes meet the hate-filled eyes of Ben, the guard from the clinic.

Calli kicks out, catching Ben in the face, his grip slipping.

"You fucking bitch!" he yells as he reaches for her again.

The thundering roar of a tiger shakes the house as Jax leaps through the open door. Ben faces the tiger and lets out his animal, the transformation from human to tiger in seconds. The tigers circle each other, snarling and swiping, each looking for a weak spot.

Lilly appears in her human form, wrapping herself in a robe left in the front bushes. She looks up at Calli, who sits at the top of the stairs and gives her a reassuring smile.

"Jax, stop playing with him," her tone bored as she leans against the doorjamb.

Jax's tiger huffs, then strikes Ben's hind quarter, drawing rivulets of blood that stream onto the floor. Ben's tiger lets out a high pitch whine as he tries to maneuver around Jax, his back leg useless.

The screeching of tires heralds Matt's arrival. He bursts in the door and grabs Ben's tiger by the scruff.

"Change!" he demands as he roughly shakes him.

In an instant, a naked, bleeding Ben cowers on the floor.

Matt's muscles bulge, his eyes a glowing turquoise blue. "Take him to the hold. We'll question him there. My wolf's too close. He needs his mate to calm him," he growls, his tone animalistic.

Jax's change is swift as he and Lilly roughly haul Ben to his feet and drag him out the door.

Taking the stairs two at a time, Matt rushes to Calli, gathering her in his arms. "It's over, baby girl. It's over," he repeat-edly whispers as he holds her tight.

Clinging to Matt, Calli lets the tears she has been holding back fall. Once again, as she's comforted by his powerful arms around her. Matt kisses her forehead, his lips lingering as he breathes in her scent.

"I have to go," he says as he reluctantly pulls back.

Calli walks Matt to the door. The lock's busted, but that can be fixed later.

"You're safe now. I need to interrogate Ben for answers. I should be back in a couple of hours." Matt's tone lowers at the thought of leaving Calli tears at him.

"I'll be fine." Calli pats his chest as she reaches up to kiss him, knowing he needs reassurance. Then she guides him out the door, closing it behind him.

CHAPTER
TWENTY-ONE

Calli walks into the kitchen and grabs a towel off the rack. Heading back towards the stairs, she cleans up the blood left behind by Ben.

Still shaken by the night's events, she spies her glass of wine and slowly makes her way to the bathroom upstairs.

Calli adds hot water to the tub and then strips off her clothes. She immerses herself in the water, letting the heat relax her tense muscles as she sips her wine.

An earth-shattering boom startles Calli out of her relaxed state, followed by sudden darkness.

Heart pounding, Calli feels around in the darkness as she carefully emerges from the tub. The creak of the floorboards to her left has her swinging in that direction just as an unimaginable pain pierces her head. She drops unconscious on the floor.

MATT STORMS into the holding cell at the town hall. The cage where Ben's chained briefly triggers memories of the blackout site when he was a child.

The cage is a good deterrent for keeping order in the town. No one wants to be reminded of that hell again.

Jax wipes his knuckles with a cloth, his blood-stained hand letting Matt know they had started without him.

"Anything yet?" Matt asks Lilly.

She shakes her head. "No, but he'll talk soon. We know how persuasive you can be."

Ben raises his swollen, bloodied face as Matt enters the cage. One eye is completely shut, with a large gash seeping blood down his cheek. Ben's half-crazed smile takes Matt by surprise.

Suddenly, the earth shakes from a resounding boom as the building descends in darkness.

Ben's maniacal laughter sends chills down their spine as he chants. "He's got her now! Vengeance! Her blood will spill just like her father spilled ours!"

Everyone stills at Ben's words. Matt looks frantically at Jax and Lilly. "CALLI!" he shouts, spurring them into action.

Leaping forward, Matt reaches for Ben in the darkness, his large hand wrapping around Ben's throat. "Who has Calli?" he growls, his wolf riding him to be let out.

Ben struggles in Matt's grip. "You'll never save her now! He will get his revenge for what her father did to him! She will become his special pet just like he was her fathers!" Ben gurgles out.

A quick intake of breath to Matt's right lets him know Lilly is close. "OH MY GOD! IT'S MAVERICK!" Lilly screams. "Maverick has her!"

Ben's acknowledging laughter cuts short as Matt snaps his neck.

TWENTY-TWO

Calli is conscious of the pain before her body slowly awakens. Keeping her eyes closed, she can feel the cool air on her naked body. Chains bite into her wrists and ankles, rough wood at her back, letting her know she's tied spread eagle against a wall.

The sound of someone approaching has her fake unconsciousness, hoping to buy more time.

"Wakey, wakey, little girl," Maverick's voice fills the room before a sharp pain explodes on her cheek when he strikes her.

Calli can't hold in the moan of pain as her head snaps to the side with force.

Maverick pinches Calli's chin, his fingers biting into her skin, shaking her. "Open your eyes, you little bitch!" he spits.

Fully alert now, Calli glares into Maverick's half-crazed gaze. "What do you want with me, Maverick?"

"What do I want? WHAT DO I WANT? I want you to feel the pain that your dear father gave me!" Maverick rants as he paces. His movements are erratic, his breathing heavy and uneven.

"M - my father?"

Whirling towards her, Maverick is inches from her face. "Yes, your father. The late, great Dr. Brent Jameson! I knew who you were the moment I caught your scent," Maverick says, tapping his nose.

"I was his 'special' boy, his pet project, so to speak. He spent many hours with me, day after day, in the cage. Always testing, torturing, breaking me, bit by bit, to study how long it would take to make me his perfect soldier."

Calli's eyes widen as she gasps, having heard some horrors her father had inflicted on the Homani.

"He's not my father," Calli says with venom. "He was the sick bastard that got my mom pregnant."

"Tomato, tomatoe." Maverick is flippant in his response. "At the end of the day, his blood runs through your veins."

Calli hears Maverick's steps as he walks away. The sound of metal ringing off metal has her imagination running wild in the darkness.

"Ah, this should do nicely."

Calli catches a glimpse of a scalpel reflecting what little light is present in the barn. With her heart pounding in her chest, Calli prays Matt will find her before Maverick takes his revenge.

"I-I thought you and Matt were close? Like brothers?" Calli stutters, buying time.

"Oh, we were at one time," Maverick chuckles at the memory. "Two little street urchins banded together to survive. Did he tell you we were both orphans?"

Quietly struggling to free herself from her chains, Calli

responds. "No. He said you were close. I just assumed you had met in the facility."

"I can hear you trying to escape, Calli. You will get extra punishment for not behaving," he says flatly, then continues. "Our parents had been drug addicts. Overdosed, I think. We lived in the same hovel, staying out of sight and stealing to survive."

Maverick gives a mirthless laugh. "We pickpocketed the wrong person. Your father, to be precise, that's how we ended up in the cages."

Maverick walks towards Calli in the darkness, bending down to eye level. The feel of cold steel on the skin above her breast has her intake a sharp breath. A surge of anger runs through her. Pulling her head back, Calli snaps it forward, stars exploding behind her eyes when she makes contact with Maverick's nose.

"YOU FUCKING BITCH!" he screams as he grabs a cloth to staunch the flow of blood.

"I'M GOING TO FUCKING KILL YOU! Slowly! Painfully!" Maverick's screams take on a high pitch gleeful tone.

"You kill me, you kill Matt! We're a mated pair, remember? You want Matt to die?" Calli appeals to him.

Maverick approaches Calli once again, this time not giving her an opportunity to lash out. As he begins slowly cutting above her breast, he whispers, "There's always a price."

Calli screams.

TWENTY-THREE

Matt's heart beats frantically in his chest as he grabs his walkie-talkie. Switching it to the general channel, he barks out a red alert to all Homani to be on the lookout for Maverick and Calli.

Knowing Maverick would hear, he ends his message with a warning.

"I'm coming for you, Maverick."

Trusting the townsfolk to leave no stone unturned, the search begins.

"Maverick's a creature of habit." Lilly begins, her brow furrowing. "He'd take her somewhere familiar to him. Somewhere with meaning."

"Holy fuck! That's it!" Jax jumps up. "He blames Calli for the cages. We have to sedate him because of his time there!"

"The barn!" They exclaim in unison.

THE THREE SHIFT as one as they hurry in animal form to the barn, praying that Calli is still alive.

The splash of icy water brings Calli out of her semi-conscious state. She can feel her warm blood dripping down her chest, combining with the coldness of the water.

Her eyelids are heavy as Calli forces them open. Maverick's face is mere inches from hers.

"Welcome back. I can't have you miss my next surprise for you," he chides her.

Maverick's walkie-talkie crackles to life. Matt's red alert and warning for him echo in the barn.

Calli's hope surges at the sound of Matt's voice. It gives her new strength, knowing that he is coming for her.

With a grunt of annoyance, Maverick picks up a thin rod, testing its flexibility.

"It seems we have less time than I would've liked." He shrugs as he draws back and lands the first blow on Calli's thigh. A welt forms immediately.

Calli closes her eyes and focuses on her love for Matt and her impending rescue. She tries to block out the excruciating pain as Maverick strikes her repeatedly.

Maverick finally relents, wiping sweat from his face as he picks up a hunting knife and approaches Calli.

Matt yips at Jax and Lilly as the barn comes into sight. He swings his head for them to go left and right. Their high pitch growls confirm they understand his intent on surrounding the barn.

Calli screams as Matt's massive black wolf bursts through the main barn doors. He takes in the sight before him.

Maverick's muscled arm is pulled back with a wicked looking knife in his hand. Calli's naked body is chained to the wall, dozens of cuts oozing blood as fresh welts rise across her hips and thighs.

The wolf lets out a deep growl as he leaps at Maverick. As they tumble together on the ground, Maverick shifts into his animal. Calli gasps at the sight of the massive grizzly bear now locked in combat with Matt's wolf.

Maverick's long fangs and razor-sharp claws swipe at the wolf, narrowly missing him. The black wolf leaps out of the way, drawing the bear closer to the other end of the barn, away from Calli.

The two deadly animals circle each other, each looking for a place to strike. A pain-filed moan from Calli distracts the wolf for a split second, allowing grizzly to strike.

As he raises his claw to swipe at the wolf's chest, Jax's tiger tackles the grizzly from the side, his long canines digging deeply into his throat.

Swiftly rolling to unseat the tiger, the bear brings his claws down on his belly, digging deep grooves within his flesh. The massive tiger hits the barn wall with a thud as the grizzly tosses him off.

Spinning toward the wolf, the bear roars, his rage feral, as he charges.

The echoing bang of a gunshot has them all going still as the bears prone form slides to a halt in front of the wolf, a gaping, bloody hole where his heart once was.

Looking at the barn door, the black wolf is shocked to see Dawn standing there with a high-powered rifle in her hand.

"First rights, Matt. First rights," Dawn whispers as she lowers the gun.

Matt and Jax change back into their human form as Dawn grabs some sweatpants from the bag in her truck that she used to follow them to the barn.

Lilly has Calli out of the chains, an old blanket covering her shoulders, mindful of her wounds. Then, carefully scooping her up in his arms, Matt rushes to Dawn's truck and gently sets Calli in the cab.

Semi-conscious, Calli moans in pain as she gently strokes Matt's face.

"You came for me," she whispers, her voice raw from screaming.

Tears fill Matt's eyes. "I'll always come for you. I'm so fucking sorry I wasn't here sooner."

"Shhh, you're here now," Calli breathes as she falls back unconscious.

TWENTY-FOUR

"C'mon on, Doc, please?" Calli begs Doc to let her out of the clinic.

It has been two weeks since the barn. Calli doesn't remember much of her time spent with Maverick. Doc suggested that this was likely Calli's mind trying to protect itself. Quite frankly, she's relieved to not have the memories. Only her scars show the hell he had inflicted on her.

Matt has told her that Maverick had blown the transformer near town to create the blackout. The loss of power is still an issue that needs to be fixed.

When Calli questioned Matt about Ben's involvement, apparently Maverick and Ben had been held in the same facility area. They had grown quite close through their mutual hatred of Dr. Brent Jameson. So it hadn't taken much for Maverick to have Ben join in on his plan. A few whispered rumours here, a promise of retribution. It had easily swayed Ben.

Matt had been relatively quiet during his discussion's of

Maverick. Calli could tell that he was mourning the loss of who Maverick had once been, and struggling with the guilt of not realising who Maverick had become. She knows that Lilly and Jax have been around to talk him through it, but she also knows firsthand that healing is a journey.

Calli is grateful to the townspeople who stop by the clinic to visit. They bring her small tokens and some apologize for believing the gossip spread by Maverick and Ben. But as of this moment, she's had enough of being treated like an invalid.

"DOC! I know you can hear me!" Calli yells once again.

A burst of laughter from the door has Calli turning in Lilly's direction. "You better be here to talk some sense into that man!" Calli wails at her friend.

Lilly walks over to the bed and drops a bag on it. "One better. I'm busting you out. Go get dressed!"

Calli jumps out of the bed, swaying briefly before she hurries into the washroom to change. Closing the door, Calli pulls the red summer dress out of the bag. At the bottom are her cowboy boots. With a squeal of delight, Calli pulls the dress over her head, the soft, stretchy material perfect comfort for her still-healing wounds.

Taking Lilly's arm, Calli and Lilly walk out the clinic doors.

Matt is leaning against his truck, his thick arms crossed, his bulging muscles on display. With a dimpled smile, he motions for Calli to twirl for him with his finger. Then, letting out a low whistle of appreciation, he opens his arms for her.

Calli saunters up to Matt, a cheeky grin on her face as she peaks at the picnic basket in front of the truck's cab. "What's going on with that?" she gestures to the basket as she walks into his waiting arms.

Giving her a gentle squeeze, Matt kisses the top of her head, rubbing his face in her hair. "Hmmm, I love your scent."

Pulling back, he grins at her. "I thought it was time I took you on an actual date. We're going for a picnic up by the lake." His eyes are shining with an unmistakable love for her.

Jax's truck has pulled up beside them. "You two lovebirds have fun," he says, catching the last part of their conversation.

"We will!" Calli beams.

"Lilly, you're in charge while we're gone," Matt addresses her.

Turning to Jax, he shakes his hand. "Jax, be safe and get home soon."

"Where's Jax going?" Calli asks with concern.

Matt watches Jax pull his truck out and head towards the gate. "He's going to Temple, a settlement south of here," Matt replies. "We heard they have a transistor there we need."

Scooping Calli up, Matt gently sits her in the truck. "Come on, my love. We have a date by the shore, and as much as I love this dress, I can't wait to take it off of you," he says as he nibbles her lip. Her mouth parts, inviting his tongue to deepen the kiss.

With a groan, Matt pulls away, his breathing rapid. "Maybe we'll save the beach for later, the house is closer," he says with urgency.

Arriving at the house, Matt scoops Calli up in his muscular arms and carries her up the stairs and into their bedroom. Slowly lowering her to the floor, their bodies rubbing as Calli's feet touch the hardwood, still wrapped in each other's arms.

Matt's lips descend on Calli's, sucking her lower lip into his mouth, his days' growth of beard rough against her skin. A soft moan leaves Calli's lips as her hands explore Matt's broad shoulders, feeling the heat of his skin under his form-fitting t-shirt. Then, leaning forward, she breaks from their kiss, biting his nipple playfully through his shirt, and their eyes meet in an invitation to do more.

With a moan, Matt lifts Calli and places her on the bed, slowly removing her dress. Staring into her eyes as he unclips her bra, her heavy breasts on display. Her scars are still an angry red. Leaning forward, Matt gently kisses each one, marvelling at her strength. Calli's pert nipples harden with desire. Matt latches his tongue around the stiffening peak, gently biting, before sucking it into his mouth. Her moan echoes through the room, her heavy breathing causing her chest to heave.

Matt turns to Calli's other nipple as he slides her boots off, his hand lightly trailing from ankle to thigh. Goosebumps rise on Calli's skin from the light touch, her desire a flush upon her skin. Then, maneuvering her onto her back, Matt kisses just below Calli's hairline at the top of her neck, his lips and tongue trailing his way down as his muscular hands caress the curvature of her spine. Then, reaching the generous globes of her ass while continuing downwards, Matt lets out a hum of approval at the sight of her creamy skin and voluptuous bounty he is massaging.

Snaking an arm underneath Calli, Matt lifts her until she is on her hands and knees in front of him. He was sparing her the weight of his body on her still-healing wounds. His broad shoulders spread her legs wide as his mouth descends on her wet pussy from behind.

Calli's back arches at the onslaught of Matt's tongue

delving deep inside her, slowly drawing back as he circles her clit. Her tension building, Calli's heartbeat stutters in her chest as she tries to catch her breath. Finally, Matt's rhythmic suction on her clit pushes her over the edge. With a high keening sound, Calli's orgasm explodes through her body as she collapses forward, weak from its intensity.

Matt's mouth devours hers, flipping her over on the bed, sharing her taste as their tongues engaged in a lovers' dance.

Lifting her forward, Matt perches Calli on the dresser. Shucking his jeans, he palms his hard length and lines himself up to her entrance. Staring into her eyes, he slides himself in, inch by torturous inch, slowly drawing out the moment.

Calli can feel the slight burn of being stretched to her limit from Matt's girth. The pleasure-pain heightens her arousal. Eyes still locked, Matt sets a leisurely pace, evoking deep moans from them both.

This wasn't sex; this was reconnecting, making love, a sharing of two souls. Wrapping her legs around Matt's hips, Calli pushes her heels into the small of Matt's back, encouraging him to increase their pace. The tightening of Calli's channel around his cock spurs on his quickening pace. Matt thrusts his hips forward, grinding deep into Calli's pussy, then pulls back, only to slam forward again and again.

Calli's eyes widen, and her mouth opens to a silent scream as the rush of her orgasm sets her body on fire. Burying his head in her shoulder, Matt's muscular hands hold firm on Calli's hips as he bucks wildly, coating her insides with his seed.

Resting their foreheads together, their labored breathing is the only sound in the room, Matt whispers. "You complete me."

EPILOGUE

J ax hates Temple. The southern town stinks with people tossing their waste in the street. The coast is littered with colonies like this one. There is no pride or honor here. No rule of law, only corruption.

Spying on the building he has been told carries transistor parts, Jax pulls up close, not wanting to leave his truck out of his sight. He's tired, cranky and not in the mood to fight.

Jax notices the doors to the shop are wide open, giving the place an airy feel. Long counters with various machinery parts line both sides of the room, with smaller shelving sporadically filling the middle.

Near the back, Jax hears voices. Rounding the shelf, he stops short at the sight of the woman working near the bench.

What the fuck?

"Calli?" Jax asks in confusion as he stares at Matt's mate. Only he knows it can't be, he just left Calli and Matt at the farm a few hours before.

Looking up from the wires she is soldering, the gorgeous redhead's eyes meet Jax. One eye is emerald green, and the other is turquoise.

BONUS CONTENT

Sometimes when I write, I will use a speech to text app on my phone. What I say, doesn't always translate properly. Maybe it's my Canadian accent? Below is a blooper scene from these sessions.

Matt Stompson to the bar, Siri how to make it store delete. Sitting at a vacant stool he jesters the bartender over, Jamison neat and keep them coming. The Young bartender raises his eyebrows at mats demeanour but knows better than to comment. Coming right up Matt he says he screws away to get mats drink. What's got you in a tizzy Jack says as he sits beside Matt clapping them on the back. Matt turns in glares at him, his eyes are bright turquoise don't fuck with me today jacks. Razee both had to surrender raising both hands in surrender, concerned that concern etching his face Jack's quietly sepsis drink give him that the time he needs. Two drinks later, Matt notices movement to his left as Lilly sits down on the on the empty barstool next one. She most sense to the bartender for vodka and tonic and then turns to Matt so you really fucked it up didn't you didn't you she says. Mats muscles bulge and his eyes flare turquoise, you just had to push it didn't you Lilly, she wasn't ready. Oh don't give me that shit Matt she was more than ready and it was way overdue for her to know the truth. Yeah well she fucking left my growls at the Lilly. Jack's leans forward what the fuck do you mean she left? She left are you both fucking deaf Matt raises his voice. The patrons in the bar quiet not used to seeing Matt so close to beast mode. Glancing around, Matt lower his voice. I told her the truth, she was petrified I told her I fucking loved her and she still laughed end of story. No somethings not right here Lily says she loves you but she does this wouldn't it just doesn't make sense. And if you loved her like you say you do you wouldn't be sitting here drowning your sorrows, you'll be out looking for because you and I both fucking know the safest place for her is here. See you boy sit here and cry in your fucking drinks and I'm gonna go do what needs to be done and find her. Lily says she gets up and walks at the bar.

Matt leans forward and breaks hands through his hair what have I done he says to jacks I love her I fucking worshiper. Jack's he's açaí he's açaí Jack's he's açaí he's Shiva oh my God delete jack lets out açaí. We knew it could happen Matt Desamor the bogeyman to others we never existed. Matt glances overheads a jacks, you didn't see her fear she couldn't wait to get away from me. Jack's clubs mad on the back you love her buddy, go find her, talk to her she'll come around she loves you too. She's your maid mate mate MATE, do you need her you need her. Matt looks at Jack's didn't even get to explain that everything just happened so fast I let my temper get the better of me and I just walked out the door I didn't explain everything. Then go, go find her explain everything if she doesn't love you like I think she loves you then there's no hope for any of us. That looks at his longtime friend thanks man I got a woman to track down Matt says he gets up to leave the bar. Go get her tiger jack sales out that turns with a smirk that would be you not me I'm a fucking wolf he says he stocks out the door.

I hear the echo delete previous paragraph. Hearing the echo of Jack's laugh as he jumps in his truck.

Sidenote when Matt walks into the bar he knows that Maverick he's sitting in the corner sipping a beer.

Kelly stands on the sidewalk looking towards town she can't bring her self to walk through knowing what she knows look into the woods to the right she decides to take the back trails to the gate to avoid running into anyone. Darkness has fallen but 3/4 moon and clear sky gives just enough light for Callie to see her way. Heart broken with tears streaming down her face Kelly sets up on the first path knowing if she stays due east she should come out to the road by the gate. The whole Mane she thinks, her joy knowing that they're alive and well is overwhelming but her fear I was the repercussions of being with them keeps her at a steady pace. Her mothers voice echos in her head, never let them find you Callie they won't understand it'll be a death sentence death sentence. Lost in her thoughts Kelly's brought to the abrupt halt by the sound of a growl hello deep growl. Looking around cautiously kelly tries to pierce through the trees to see what's making that sound. A twig snaps to your left call Macaulay whips around see nothing but shadows. Moving to her right she has the feeling of being hunted. She knows there's no wild animals in these words is they belong to the Hamani and they are the Apex predator predators predators. Whatever's out there it's her money it's Omani. Fear rising from her valley Kelly takes off at a fast run branches and thorns tearing at her skin and clothing clothing. The sounds of a heavy gallop getting closer behind her. Drop Callie Lily yells as she leaps in the air morphing into a panther and landing with a heavy third third THUD. Covering her mouth with both hands to keep from screaming, Callie is in shock by witnessing how many change. The Lily Panther quietly stocks 3 feet into the woods and let's out a deafening roar. She's protecting me, holy shit, stairs an hour kelly stairs an hour stairs in awe STARESINAWE is lily in panther form stands guard. Minutes the felt like hours pass by before the Lily panther turns to Cali and slowly walks towards her. Stopping only a few feet away, lily chefs back into a human form. Are you OK? Lilly asks Lilly asks. I am I am kelly stutters in shock. Approaching her slowly Lily nails down to her Calias on the ground are you hurt? I know now I think I'm I think I'm just in shock kelly answers. Lily smiles her turquoise eyes still shining bright she holds her hand to Cali. Hi I'm Lilly and I'm a hoe Manny panther nice to meet you she chuckles chuckles. Taking Lilly's headed hers as Lily helps her off the ground Callie gives her a ride smile I'm Cali human nice to meet you she replies and they both burst out in laughter. Glancing back at the woods, who was that or what was that? Kelly inquires to Lily two. I'm not sure who it was Kelly, I didn't pick up their scent they were too far away I could probably go on track but I don't wanna leave you alone. Lily response.

Callie and Lily worked her way back through the trail

towards the main house. And mats truck comes to a screeching halt as he jumps out and rushes up to Callie and Lily. Oh I was looking for you everywhere Matt says I couldn't find you anywhere in town are you OK? Matt says his hands open and close like he wants to reach for her.

I hope you enjoyed reading these bloopers as much as I did!
　- Sarren

ALSO BY SARREN SCRIBNER

<u>**Homani Series**</u>

Homani Tried (Book One)

Homani Tested (Book Two)

Homani True (Book Three) - Coming Fall 2023

ABOUT THE AUTHOR

Canadian GenX grandma who loves writing smut. Mostly found in her pajamas, with a coffee in one hand and a book or laptop in the other. 'Covered in dog hair' is her new fashion trend.

Find more information about me and my books at
www.sarrenscribner.com

www.ingramcontent.com/pod-product-compliance
Lightning Source LLC
Chambersburg PA
CBHW051807050726

47598CB00006B/2459